Nor Will You Escape

Sebastian Vaughan

Clapham Press

Published by
Clapham Press
40 Voltaire road,
London SW4 6DH

www.claphampress.co.uk

First Edition
First Published 2010

Copyright © Robin Vickery 2010

Designed by Eleanor Maclure
Set in Garamond
Cover image 'I Walk Alone'
www.istockphoto.com

Printed by Marston Book Services Ltd
Abingdon, Oxfordshire
www.marston.co.uk

ISBN 978-0-9565753-0-2

*"Hurry as fast as you can,
yet you will never arrive,
Nor will you escape by running away"*

Ecclesiasticus chapter 11 verse 10

Chapter 1

It was getting dark outside now and the room was gloomy. Somebody got up, walked over to the door and flicked the light switch, and rows of fluorescent tubes buzzed into life, filling the large open-plan office with their harsh and unnatural brilliance.

He took a pen out of his pocket and wrote something totally meaningless on his copy of the agenda. About ten or fifteen minutes, he thought. Then it would be over and he could get home to the bottle of Chardonnay he'd left in the fridge. Should be nicely chilled by now. He felt the first twinges of cramp in his right leg, which was crossed over his left, and shifting on the uncomfortable plastic chair he stretched the leg in front of him, barely suppressing a yawn as he did so.

He always found these Area Forum meetings unbearably tedious. And to make things worse, there was no reason to think they actually achieved anything. Their sole purpose, as far as he could see, was to give the local worthies an opportunity to posture in front of each other and exchange the same well-worn platitudes mixed in with professional jargon, so that they could at least feel their existence was justified. You cynical bastard, he thought.

But this meeting had been more interesting than some he had been to. He'd spent most of it looking across the circle of chairs to where she was sitting, directly opposite him. She'd not been to one of these meetings before, he thought. If she had, there was no way he would have failed to notice her.

He guessed she was aged around thirty. Her dark eyes were large and beautiful. Her nose was turned up just enough to be disarmingly cute and her mouth was wide and sensuous. Her thick light-brown hair fell untidily over her shoulders, with a few rebellious strands drifting across her smooth, pale cheeks. There was perhaps the merest trace of make-up on her face. Her unvarnished fingernails were cut short.

The faded pink T-shirt stretched itself across her full and rounded breasts and her navel peered invitingly over the waistband of impossibly tight blue denim jeans that were split at both knees. Her bare feet were encased in worn leather moccasins that looked as though they might have been very expensive when they were new.

Several times during the meeting he'd had to drop his gaze before she caught him looking, and now he pretended to be making notes again on his agenda. In fact he was thinking how much he wanted to pour clear golden honey over her naked body and spend the rest of that night slowly licking it off.

The Reverend Gavin Piers Jonathan Salter, rector of St Mary the Virgin, Hadleigh Bridge, with St John the Evangelist, Lower Barsham and priest-in-charge of St Peter's, Wimhurst was much too fond of alcohol, felt periodically guilty about his sexual behaviour and had never fully recovered from the lonely and oppressive years spent at an exclusive boarding school. Somewhere inside his head, a small nagging voice told him his conversion to high-church Anglicanism at university had been nothing more than an over-sophisticated protest, and although he managed to ignore it most of the time, it occasionally edged him towards depression. His long-separated parents had lost no time in deriding his vocation to the priesthood as soon as they heard about it, accusing him of being self-centred and having no consideration for them. And when his reclusive and alcoholic mother had died of liver disease, his father, with utter predictability, had put the blame for her death squarely on him. And just to underline his condemnation of his only son, he had redrafted his will leaving most of his wealth to one of Gavin Salter's cousins. When a few years later his father had dropped dead from overwork, high blood pressure and too many business lunches, Salter should have been free at last from it all. But the same small voice had told him that if only he had done things differently, things might have turned out differently.

Looking on the positive side, which he usually managed to do, there was a sense of fulfilment in his work which told him it was right for him. And though he had never found faith easy, he somehow could not bring himself to believe there was nothing. All of which meant he could carry on being the local priest without feeling he was too much of a fraud.

Gavin Salter was thirty-seven years old and, in spite of his dislike of exercise and mildly unhealthy diet, was in reasonable shape. From somewhere in the generations of his family he had inherited dark and classically male good looks, though he wore them with a dissolute and somewhat jaded air. He was fortunate that the uniform of his profession suited him well and even gave him a certain flair, and being single with no financial responsibilities beyond his own needs, his clergy stipend was enough to provide him with an off-duty wardrobe of good quality clothes. Being a bit of a loner, the solitude of a small country town like Hadleigh Bridge suited him and he rarely if ever felt it was closing in on him, as some priests might have done in his situation. So his estimate of himself was that he had arrived safely without having suffered too much damage on the way, and was therefore as near to being happy as he was likely to be, at least in this life.

The meeting came to an end and the Director of Social Services thanked everyone with his usual condescending manner and reminded them when the next meeting was. Salter made a note in his diary. He stood up, folded his agenda and minutes and put them into the inside pocket of his jacket. Then he casually crossed the room. After a formal handshake and a brief conversation, his curiosity was satisfied. Her name was Catherine Laurence and she had recently taken up post as the new Senior Social Worker.

He walked down the stairs of the Social Services building and across the empty car park to his car. It was a mild evening and he was relieved when the ageing vehicle started first time. It didn't always. As he pulled into the main road, he thought how he had always liked the name Catherine. Ahead of him the sun was setting over Hadleigh Bridge and the sky was an explosion of pink and orange.

Now he was ready for that cold Chardonnay.

Chapter 2

The man sitting alone at the corner table looked at his watch for the third time in two minutes. Where the hell is that idiot? he thought. The restaurant was crowded and the large dining room was vibrant with conversation and the clatter of tableware. The white-jacketed waiters flitted back and forth across the room, disappearing through the swing door to the kitchen and reappearing with plates of the very best French cuisine.

He slipped his hand into the side pocket of his jacket and fingered the packet of Marlboro and the gold electronic lighter. It was almost a caress. Damn this ridiculous smoking ban, he thought. God, he was dying for a cigarette. He hated waiting for people who were late and not being able to smoke was making it worse. In any case, professionals couldn't afford to be late. Not in their line of business. Being late could be dangerous.

His mobile throbbed quietly.

"I'm near you. Give me about five minutes. Train was delayed. Why don't you order? I'm happy to eat whatever's going. I'm sure it'll be great. Heck, I'm really hungry".

"Will do", said the man, and he ended the call and gestured

to one of the waiters who'd been hovering discretely for several minutes now.

The man was of Eastern European appearance and he had just the hint of a tan. A band of thick dark hair encircled his otherwise bald head and a heavy black moustache completely covered his top lip. He looked to be in his middle forties.

The black jacket and dark-grey slacks fitted his lean body as only expensive tailor-made garments can and the cream silk shirt was set off perfectly by the red and blue patterned tie. His brown casuals were unmistakably hand-made and the heavy gold Rolex watch completed the overall impression of quality, style and taste, and sufficient money to pay for them.

The waiter leaned over him, pad and pen in hand, scribbling rapidly as he ordered fish hors d'oeuvres, main dishes of meat, a bottle of Sancerre Blanc and one of Beaujolais Villages. He was about to look at his watch again when the other man arrived.

"Hi! How are you?" said the new arrival in a soft and cultured American accent. "Really sorry I'm late". They could have been colleagues at the office, who met for dinner all the time and played golf at the weekends. Or old friends who'd known each other for years and now couldn't wait to catch up on all the gossip and the scandal. In fact, they had never even seen each other before that moment.

The other man looked the stereotypical business executive. Well cut, off-the-peg mid-grey suit, pale blue button-down-collar shirt, unremarkable tie held neatly in place with a clip, meticulously polished black loafers. His hair was short and bristly, almost but not quite the classic nineteen-fifties crew cut, and together with the closely shaven face and rimless spectacles, it gave him the air of a clean-living, thirty-something family man.

"So, how's the accommodation? Are they looking after you?" asked the other man, as the waiter served the hors d'oeuvres and filled their glasses with the chilled Sancerre.

The question sounded normal enough and it was meant to. It was unlikely that anyone was listening to their conversation and even less likely that it was being analysed, but in their kind of work it was always best to be safe. The American was not interested whether the first man was satisfied with his accommodation or not. Only that he had checked into the hotel as arranged and was now fully equipped and ready to embark on the mission for which he had been trained and briefed over a period of weeks.

"Everything's fine", said the man. His English pronunciation was impeccable and the accent was faint and barely noticeable.

"The hotel's very comfortable. And it's not too far from the station, I'm pleased to say". With these words he informed his companion that he was fully prepared and that early the next morning he would be traveling by Eurostar from the Gare du Nord, Paris to London, St Pancras.

"Now that's what I wanna hear," said the other man, smiling broadly and sounding very American. "By the way, here's that stuff I promised you. I know you've really been itching to take a look at this". He opened a slim, leather briefcase and took out a brown envelope. Then he passed it across the table. It could have been a company report showing last year's profits. But, as the first man knew, it contained maps and train times for his journey on from London, a detailed description of the person he had already contacted from the organisation's safe house in

Paris and was now due to meet the following day, and a large amount of carefully researched background information.

"Thanks for this. I'll take a good look at it later," said the man, and slipped the envelope into the inside pocket of his jacket. "Now, how about you? What have you been getting up to lately?" Once again, the question seemed innocent. But, as they both knew, it was the signal for the other man to produce from the briefcase a number of colour photographs. The first man looked at them one by one, and in spite of the trivial small talk they were both making, he was studying them carefully and memorizing their contents. Then he handed them back to the other man, because he knew that under no circumstances could he carry them with him.

The meal was over now. The American paid the bill with an unobtrusive credit card, and they stood up from the table, shaking hands and smiling at each other warmly. They had done what they had come there to do. Then they left the restaurant separately.

The first man lit a Marlboro, inhaled the smoke deeply and walked at a leisurely pace along a street lined with pavement cafés. He liked Paris. He remembered the last time he had been here. That was three years before. Just after he had joined the organization. But England. That was a different matter. He had never liked the English. He thought how much he resented having to go there the next morning. But then this was work, not a holiday.

He got onto the Metro and made a long and circuitous journey to his hotel, changing trains several times. He always did that in large cities. It had become a habit with him. Just in case he was being followed.

He unlocked the door of his room at the hotel, took his jacket off and hung it on the back of a chair. He poured a cognac from the mini-bar. Only a small one. He would need a clear head the next day. In the bathroom, he splashed cold water on his face, brushed his teeth and rinsed his mouth with a sharp mouthwash. Then he turned the light out, undressed and got into bed. He lay for some time in the darkened room thinking about the photographs he had seen. Running the details through his mind helped him remember them.

They were photographs of a church called St Mary the Virgin, in a small English country town called Hadleigh Bridge.

Chapter 3

Gavin Salter ran the tip of his finger lightly down the inside of Catherine Laurence's left thigh, pausing briefly to stroke the erogenous zone at the back of her knee, then continuing down her calf to her ankle. Then he cradled her foot in both his hands, lifting it gently to his mouth and flicking his tongue between her toes. She giggled softly.

"That tickles", she said, her voice muffled by the pillow in which her face was buried.

"It's meant to", he said, and kissed the sole of her foot. Then bending over, he bit into the soft flesh around her waist.

"Ouch! You pervert!" she screamed and brought the flat of her hand down with a crack onto his shoulder blade. He seized her with both arms and they rolled over, and for the next minute they explored each other's mouth in a lingering kiss.

The morning after the Area Forum meeting, Salter had got her telephone number from the Director of Social Services and had rung her on the pretext of "networking". He'd discovered she had moved only recently into the area and had taken up her post less than three weeks before, so he'd felt he needed no excuse to invite her out to lunch. That had been followed a few days later by dinner at a restaurant not far from the village, and afterwards, over coffee and brandy in the rectory's large, oak-paneled sitting room, their first sexual encounter had taken place.

His initial assessment of her at the meeting had in no way prepared him for the stunning beauty of her naked body and the overpowering attraction he would feel for her. There was something animal about her. The scent of her was pure and at the same time intoxicating. It made him think of grass and forests. Her stomach and waistline, permanently suggesting the early stages of pregnancy, would have had some women reaching frantically for their diet sheets, and she had just the hint of a double chin. But she was clearly confident about the way she looked. And in any case he wouldn't have changed anything about her. Her broad, uninhibited smile, the way she bit her lower lip when something puzzled her and her habit of chewing the end of her thumb all endeared her to him irresistibly.

And to his added delight, he found they had a number of things in common. She loved the sunset. She refused to do anything in the morning until a large mug of steaming hot tea had been put into her hand. She was suspicious of anything that looked vaguely institutional. She liked the peace and quiet of museums and art galleries, and she was incurably addicted to Italian food.

It was late afternoon, on a warm Monday in early September. She had taken the half-day that was owed to her and he had decided the article for the parish news sheet could wait. And after a few glasses of champagne and sandwiches from the delicatessen in the high street, they had spent almost four hours in bed.

"So, are we having an affair?" she said, running her fingers down his spine and stroking his lower back.

"Yeah, I guess we are" he said, stretching lazily and thoroughly enjoying what she was doing to him.

"And what would the Bishop think of that, Father?" And lifting herself on one elbow, she looked at him with the wide-eyed gaze he had already become so fond of.

He sighed, deeply and thoughtfully. "Well in the first place it's none of his business, because it's not affecting my work as a priest. And secondly, I don't happen to think love is a sin. If it is then I'm in the wrong religion."

"That sounds alright". She hugged him and kissed his neck.

He rolled onto his back. "Mind you, I'd be worried if any of my parishioners found out. Or at least the ones who wouldn't approve."

"They won't find out from me, that's for sure. I'm a social worker, remember? Everything's confidential. Tell me, why did you use the word 'love'?"

"Well … I guess … love is what we're doing … isn't it? I mean … I like to think it's got at least some sort of meaning to it. You know, it's not like we're just screwing".

"Felt awfully like it to me", she said and grinned.

"You know what I'm trying to say. It can't just be for my gratification. Not with me being … you know … what I am. If it was, then I shouldn't really be doing it at all. It's got to … kind of … well, mean something to me in terms of what I believe in."

"Great. Now I'm a theological concept". And she stuck her thumb in her mouth.

"Shut up!" he said and dug the fingers of one hand into her ribs. She screamed and giggled.

"I know I'm not making a very good job of this, but what I mean is that I really like you and I'm enjoying getting to know you. And so I don't feel bad about what we're doing. I mean, I don't think it's wrong. And I reckon what we have could be something really good, if that's what we both want and we both feel right about it."

She slipped her arms around his neck and drew him close to her, brushing his cheek with her lips.

"That was lovely of you to say that and I really appreciate it. But we've only known each other a couple of weeks, so I don't have any expectations at all. And I don't want you to feel you have to commit unless, like you say, it's what you really want and you feel right about it."

He held her soft, warm body against his. He didn't say anything, but just looked deep into her eyes. He felt embarrassed at his stumbling efforts to explain how he felt. But he was very happy holding her. Happier maybe than he'd been for some time.

Their mouths came together in a kiss, and for the second time that day they made love passionately.

An hour later they were in the kitchen. Salter, wearing a dark-blue cotton dressing gown, was standing at the sink washing the ingredients for a salad. She was sitting on a wooden chair, wearing the black clerical shirt that had fallen to the floor when they had undressed that afternoon. The shirt was unbuttoned and her bare legs were splayed across the kitchen table.

"Can I come to your church some time? I'll be discreet, I promise."

Salter shook the water off a handful of lettuce leaves.

"Everyone's welcome in God's house, discreet or otherwise.

But didn't you tell me you used to go?"

"Mmm, I did. Mum and Dad were pretty regular and they always took me with them. So I grew up with it really. Then when I was fourteen I got confirmed, so I guess I've done the whole bit."

"So what happened?"

"The usual thing. I was the classic drifter. University was a long way from home and none of the friends I made ever went near a church. And I used to sleep in on Sundays. You know how it is".

He dried his hands. Opening the fridge door he took out two large steaks wrapped in paper, took the paper off and laid them on a board beside the cooker.

"But how about the believing side of it? Does that still make sense?"

"Sure it does. Makes a whole lotta sense".

"So you just need to pick up the threads". He reached across the table and gently squeezed her knee. "Come on, make yourself useful. The salad needs dressing. Potatoes are in the oven and they'll be ready soon." He poured olive oil into an enormous frying pan, heated it over the gas and threw the steaks in, adding garlic cloves, black pepper and herbs. For the next ten minutes they sizzled, filling the kitchen with a delicious aroma.

At first, they ate the meal in silence, which gave Salter the opportunity to look at her again. She looked thoughtful and even preoccupied. But from the way she cut purposefully into the steak and quickly emptied her first glass of the rich, red wine, he could see she was enjoying it. He felt relaxed in her company, as if he didn't have to prove anything or justify anything, and he hoped she felt the same. He refilled their glasses.

"So what made you come to Hadleigh Bridge?" he said.

"I'm not really sure". She put her knife and fork down and picked up her wine glass. "I'm already wondering if I've done the right thing. I spent so many years in London, and it was always in the most deprived areas. I used to feel like an inner-city person and I never thought I'd be anything else. But then one day I really felt I needed to move on, and I started worrying that if I didn't I'd just get stuck and that would be it for the rest of my life. Then I saw this job advertised in the paper and something just clicked. I applied for it and got it and here I am".

She put the glass down and for a moment there was silence again.

"Anyway," she said, "tell me what it's like around here. See if you can convince me I've done the right thing".

Salter leaned back in his chair. "Blue-rinse brigade. Second-home weekenders. City bankers who prefer to commute. Wealthy retired. A few Tory-voting natives who think what's happened to the place is dreadful. Small upmarket council estate, kids go to the nearby comprehensive. Picture-postcard village green. No serious social problems. The odd antique shop. One Chinese takeaway. Enough stereotypes for you?"

"I get the picture," said Catherine, holding a large piece of steak on the end of her fork. "So what keeps you here?"

"The fact that two days are never the same. Sure, certain days have their jobs, like doing the Sunday service sheet on Saturdays. But I never know who I'm going to meet when I go out, or who it'll be when I pick up the phone. I get close to people. A priest does. And sometimes I can be some use to them. And if I need my own space, I can usually find it. The pace of modern living hasn't quite hit Hadleigh Bridge yet. At least not with full force."

She chewed the end of her thumb. "Don't you ever get lonely?" she said.

"I think I'm probably lonely all the time. It's just that I happen to like it. And if it ever gets to me, I've got one or two old friends not far away. I don't see them very often but we keep in touch. Just about."

Catherine frowned slightly. Then she looked at him and smiled. It was a warm and caring smile.

"So tell me a bit about these three churches of yours. St Mary's is the parish church, isn't it? What's the Sunday morning service like?"

"Well, we're of the anglo-catholic tradition. "High Church", some people call it. Which means I wear vestments and we burn incense and do it all in a ceremonial kind of way. It's very beautiful and it's always appealed to me. I'm sure you must have come across it."

Catherine nodded thoughtfully. "Yes, I have. Although my church at home wasn't like that at all. But I reckon I could get into it if I went to church again. I quite like the idea of rituals and ceremonies. It all has a kind of ... I dunno ... mystery about it. Symbols carry a lot of meaning. Much more than words do".

She frowned slightly again. "But what about women being ordained? Priests like you object to it, don't they?"

"Well, some of us do". He emptied his glass. "But I've never had a problem with it".

"So you never thought about leaving the Church of England

or anything like that. I remember reading that a lot of priests had done".

"That's right. And some of them became Roman Catholic. Others stayed around and carried on as if nothing had happened and refused to accept the change. And the rest of us ... well, change happens and sometimes it's the right thing. If you look at the history of the Church, there's always been change of some kind."

She held her empty glass out for refilling. "Do you know what's always been my problem with religion? It seems to be more into its own preservation than anything else. I mean, I've worked in neighbourhoods where there's been real poverty and real need. And the church is just this ugly building up the road that's locked all week and gets opened on Sunday so that a handful of better-off people can file in and out again. And the vicar's never seen in the worst parts. Except when someone dies. Sorry, I'm being negative aren't I?"

"Carry on". He poured the last of the wine into her glass and then into his own. "This is nothing I haven't heard before."

"Okay. At least you're listening and I appreciate that." And as she spoke, he felt her bare foot touching his.

"I've always known who I can turn to for help in my work, and they haven't always been religious, not by any means. Some of them thought it was all rubbish. But they were the ones who'd spend till three in the morning with someone who was threatening to kill themselves or who was on a downer from heroin. Or maybe they'd give up their leave to take a special-needs group away on a holiday. I mean, anyone can say they believe in something or other. But what's the point if you're not trying to be of some use?"

She emptied her glass and put it down.

"So? Tell me I'm talking crap."

"You're not. I used to say exactly the same myself and I still find myself thinking it sometimes. But, you know, faith is all about the question Why? Unless you believe in God, you can't answer that question. Without faith, there's no meaning. None whatever. And if everything is meaningless, then what does it matter whether people care about each other or not? And why bother with justice and stuff like that? There's no point, because in the end it all comes down to absolutely nothing."

Catherine chewed the end of her thumb. "Yeah," she said, and stared down at the surface of the kitchen table. "Yeah. You're absolutely right. People need faith in God. And they need faith in each other. You can't separate the two."

She leaned her head on one hand and ran her finger round the rim of the empty glass.

"Let's see," he said. "Shall I get some dessert?"

She raised her eyes and smiled at him. "I thought you were the dessert" she said sleepily. And standing up, she let the black clerical shirt slip from her naked body and fall to the floor. Then she walked round the table and eased herself cat-like onto his lap, drawing her legs up and nuzzling her face into his neck.

"I guess we're in for an early night," he said, stroking her body and feeling the coolness of her skin. "I've got a service at ten, and then I've got some work to do on a sermon. And in the afternoon some guy's coming to see me."

"Anyone important?" she said, softly biting his earlobe.

"Could be. He comes from Slovakia."

"Very impressive". She slipped her hand inside his dressing

gown and ran the tips of her fingers over his stomach. "So what's that all about?"

"I'm not certain," he said, kissing the top of her head and breathing the scent of her hair. "He's from some educational institute. Said something about historical research. All a bit vague, really."

"Well, I'm sure you'll sort him out. But you need to get a good night's sleep first." And gently turning his head, she thrust her tongue deep into his mouth.

Chapter 4

The Eurostar from Paris slid lazily into the terminal at St Pancras and came to a halt. The man folded the Herald Tribune and put it on the empty seat next to him, craning his neck to catch a glimpse of the network of steel girders which arched overhead. So this is their new Eurostar terminal. Very impressive, he thought cynically. He fingered the packet of Marlboro in his jacket pocket. It would still be a while before he was able to smoke and he drummed his fingers impatiently on the table in front of him.

He had changed his outfit of the previous night for a conservative grey double-breasted suit and plain dark-blue tie. He always carried at least one change of clothes when he was on assignments, because it made tracking him more difficult. And because he liked clothes. He had, of course, developed the art of packing the outfits into a comparatively small suitcase. A smaller case attracted less attention and made it easier for him to move quickly if he needed to. He got off the train and walked at a relaxed pace along the platform, wheeling the case behind him, and took the escalator to ground level. On the other side of the automatic doors, the station hall was teeming with people. He headed for the brick archways that led to the underground. Then briefly glancing at a map of the network displayed on a wall, he reminded himself of the route he needed to take. He had, of course, memorized it before leaving Paris, but it was always best to make certain. He never left anything to chance. Not even such a simple matter as a short journey on the London Underground. He bought a ticket from the machine.

He got off at Waterloo and took the escalator up to the main station, looking casually at his watch. The journey had been carefully researched, so he knew he had exactly thirty-five minutes before his train left. He was in good time. He bought a ticket at the ticket office. Then looking up at the information board, he verified the time of the train and noted the platform number. At left luggage he deposited the suitcase, having first unzipped a side pocket and removed a flat leather document case.

He bought a large black coffee at one of the cafés and sat down at an empty table. He really needed a smoke.

It was several months now since he had been home and he was beginning to resent the fact. First it had been that business in Iraq. Then it was the drugs shipment for the Russians. And now it was this. He remembered how close he had come to turning it down, particularly when he had realized how big the whole thing was. And how dangerous. He'd even thought of getting out altogether. There was money in the Swiss bank account and he had the flat in Berlin, so he'd be alright. And there would always be one-off jobs for him somewhere in the world. Jobs he could take or leave.

But he'd decided it wasn't worth getting on the wrong side of the organization. Too risky. They could make things difficult for him. They could even dispense with him altogether, the way they always did when they decided someone was no more use to them. So he had agreed and taken the assignment. One day he would retire comfortably. But for now he worked for them. After all, he stood to make a lot of money out of this one. And it would take him home, to Slovakia. At least for a while.

He checked his watch again. It was time. He walked across the station hall, through the barrier and onto the platform. He found a carriage that was nearly empty and took a seat by the window. Then he unzipped the document case and took out the papers that the other man had given him in the restaurant the previous night. He had already gone through them thoroughly on the journey from Paris. Now he just needed to check he knew it all.

The train pulled out of the station, and trundled through the suburbs of South London and into the countryside of Surrey and Hampshire.

He looked out of the window and tried to imagine the person he was about to meet. He hadn't been given any photographs of him, only a brief description, so he didn't really know what he looked like. And there was very little information on him. Which wasn't surprising, he thought. The organisation didn't keep files on people unless they were important. That would be a waste of time. There were too many key people to keep tabs on, like the politicians and the industrialists. This guy was basically a nobody and the main thing was getting him to co-operate. And if he wasn't convinced and didn't want to go along with it ... well, then there would be the contingency plan. An accident would be organised, somewhere close to where he lived, so that the national press didn't get hold of it.

Maybe in his own house. Burglars or something. He would have to move quickly on that one, before the guy had time to talk to anyone else. A call to head office and they'd take care of it, probably within a few hours, a day at the most. Then he would catch a plane to somewhere like Spain or Italy and hold up in another of the organisation's safe houses for a few days and await instructions.

But it was going to work. He would make sure it did. He had never failed at his job.

The slow train stopped at every station along the line, and he made a careful note of their names in a small loose-leaf notebook. The others could need an escape route at any time and one of these small towns and villages might have to provide it.

He changed trains. Once again he found a nearly empty carriage and sat by the window. Just occasionally the countryside reminded him of Slovakia. But he still didn't like England, or the English. Which was good, he thought. Because it would make it that much easier to do the job. Not that he would have had any conscience about doing the job anyway. There was no place for conscience. Not in his line of work.

The train pulled into the next station. It was Hadleigh Bridge.

Chapter 5

"Grant that by the power of your Holy Spirit, and according to your holy will, these gifts of bread and wine may be to us the body and blood of our Lord Jesus Christ."

Gavin Salter made the sign of the cross over the silver-plated chalice and paten and thought back to that moment just after seven when he had woken up next to Catherine. Her head was on his chest and he could feel her warm breath. Strands of her hair were in his mouth. Their legs were entangled.

"This is my blood of the new covenant ... do this, as often as you drink it, in remembrance of me."

They had fallen into bed and made love for the third time that day and the simultaneous orgasm had left them both exhausted, their bodies stuck to each other with sweat. And the last thing he remembered before floating into a deep and dreamless sleep was Catherine reaching out with one hand and pulling the duvet over them.

"As our Saviour has taught us, so we pray ... Our Father, who art in heaven .. "

His previous relationships had left him feeling guilty and self-justifying. But this time he was getting none of that. Just a growing sense that, from now on, his life would be incomplete if Catherine wasn't in some way part of it. And that was a bit worrying, he thought as he placed his hands on the edge of the altar and genuflected.

"This is the Lamb of God, who takes away the sins of the world ... "

What would they make of it? he wondered, as he looked down the church at the five people who always came to the ten o'clock Tuesday Eucharist. Would they think he was sinning? One or two of them might. Others would smile and put a hand on his shoulder and tell him he needed the companionship. And someone would make the inevitable joke about vicars' wives.

"The Body of Christ."

The wooden communion rail groaned and creaked as one by one they knelt down and leaned against it. He pressed the small, circular wafers into the palms of the open hands and heard the whispered amens. She'd said she would ring him that evening and he knew that whatever he did for the rest of the day, he would be thinking about her. And he guessed that his impatience would eventually get the better of him and that he'd be the one who would ring.

"The peace of God which passes all understanding keep your hearts and minds ... and the blessing of God Almighty, the Father, the Son and the Holy Spirit ... "

With the blade of his hand he traced an imaginary cross in the air. Another one over, he thought. And once again he'd played the role. Same as he always did. Maybe they'd been right. Those friends at college who'd told him he was just on an ego trip. Maybe he should have listened to them.

For a moment he felt the depression returning, like an old but unwanted acquaintance. He pushed it to the back of his mind. Three of the tiny congregation had left hurriedly, as they always did. He spent a few minutes making superficial conversation with the other two, his mind completely elsewhere. In the sacristy he unbuttoned his alb and slipped it off, hanging it carefully on a wire coat hanger on the back of the door. Then he washed the chalice and paten and dried them, put them in the safe and filled in the service register. Locking the main door, he walked slowly back to the rectory.

The bedroom was as they had left it, pillows scattered around and the duvet on the floor. He couldn't help smiling to himself as he noticed the scanty black lace knickers on the bedside table next to the alarm clock. In the kitchen, he picked up the clerical shirt and threw it over the back of a chair. Then he washed the frying pan, put the plates and glasses in the dishwasher, filled the kettle and switched it on. When it boiled, he made dark roast coffee in the cafetière, filled a large mug and took it with him into the small ground-floor room he used as a study. Sitting down at his desk, he switched the computer on and opened the file which was his half-completed sermon for the following Sunday. Barely concentrating, he read over what he had written.

Was he in love with Catherine? For a moment, he could feel the cynic in him coming out. What was this in-love thing? Was it all a creation of post-war Hollywood? Something to write schmaltzy songs about to distract Western audiences from the inherent problems of capitalism? No, he decided. There must be something in it. He'd been close to it himself once or twice. Or so he'd thought at the time.

But did he want someone else in his life? Being alone was his thing and it had suited him fine. Up to now he'd been happy that way. Was he really prepared to give it up? Would he end up wanting his life back? And would he come to resent her for taking it away from him?

In any case, how did he know he could trust her? Looking back on it, he could see he'd never really trusted any of the women he'd been with. He'd never wanted to risk it. Now here was someone who could hurt him. Someone who, if he was not very careful, could destroy everything he had built up around himself and then leave him sitting in the wreckage. And what sort of a priest would he be then? Could he really afford to take that chance?

Then again, what if he ended up hurting her? So far, he'd always managed to avoid doing that to anyone. Suppose everything went badly wrong, and all because he had lowered his guard and let her in. It might stay with him for years. Maybe for the rest of his life. Could he live with that?

But in spite of everything the logical side of his brain was telling him, he couldn't deny the way he felt about her. It was becoming clearer every minute. And he knew, with a disturbing degree of certainty, that he had never felt this way about anyone before. Maybe there had been a stage at which he could have stopped it before it went any further. But although he had only met her a short time ago, he was sure that stage was already past. Now he would have to destroy it to stop it. And in the process of doing that, he might well be destroying something in himself.

He looked at his watch. Ten to midday. Had he really been sitting there an hour? He'd done nothing to the sermon beyond a couple of sentences and a few amendments. So that's a late session tonight, he thought. Or tomorrow night. Unless he was seeing Catherine. And suddenly he tasted her mouth and tongue and felt her fingernails raking the length of his back. God, what was the matter with him?

He closed the file and shut the computer down, then went upstairs to the bedroom. He picked up the duvet and the pillows and made the bed. Then he retrieved the lace knickers from the bedside table and dropped them into the linen basket. "Go on! Sniff them, you weirdo! You know you want to!" said Catherine's voice inside his head. He hung up some clothes in the wardrobe and straightened the curtains. It was nearly time for lunch and he was hungry.

The cold tin of beer hissed at him as he pulled the ring. There was ham in the fridge and leftover salad from their meal, so he cut two thick slices of crusty white bread and made a sandwich with plenty of mayonnaise. Then he sat down at the kitchen table and read the Guardian while he ate and drank.

Articles about global warming and the pensions crisis managed to get his mind off Catherine and drinking beer at that hour of the day was having a soporific effect. He yawned and stretched and consumed the last mouthful of the sandwich, making a mental note to get some more of that ham from the deli. He emptied the rest of the beer into his glass and downed it in one. He felt good and thought about getting another beer. Perhaps he shouldn't. He liked a drink, but so far he'd kept it within limits. Well, most of the time. Then something made him look at his watch.

Shit, he thought. Five to two and the guy was due at two. He sprang off the chair and threw the glass and plate into the dishwasher. Then he bounded up the stairs, tripping onto the landing and cursing to himself. In the bathroom he splashed cold water on his face and brushed his teeth, checking himself in the mirror and running a hand through his hair. He looked alright, he thought. Then he took a deep breath and let it slowly out.

As he reached the bottom of the stairs, the doorbell rang. He crossed the hall and opened the rectory's heavy oak door.

"Father Gavin Salter?" said the man.

Chapter 6

Catherine Laurence swallowed down her third cup of black coffee and searched her desk drawer for the paracetamol. She was regretting having drunk so much, even if it had been worth it.

On the subject of regret, she wasn't at all sure she'd made the right decision in coming to Hadleigh Bridge. It was green, leafy and peaceful and you could certainly leave your car parked without expecting to find the wheels had been removed when you came back. But the novelty of all that was beginning to wear off. Most of the people she worked with were great and she'd made some good friends in the office. But some of them were really Victorian in their attitudes and thought they had the right to be condescending while they dished out charity to poor needy souls. And even though she'd only been there a few weeks, it was already beginning to get her down.

Still, she thought, it wasn't her job to sort out the system or the attitudes of those who ran it. Not if she was going to stay there for any length of time. In any case, her headache was bad enough without an attack of work-related depression on top of it.

She checked her emails for the second time that morning.

There was nothing from him, but then she wasn't really expecting anything, as they'd agreed that talking on the phone was better and safer. So she'd ring him that evening. Or should she leave it and let him ring her? No, she wasn't into playing games. She would ring him, just like she'd said she would. But not too late, so there would still be time for a drink at the local if neither of them was doing anything. Then back to his place again? Or her flat, maybe, for a change?

"Have you got the Norwood file?" The voice interrupted her thoughts and she snapped back to reality.

"Sorry?"

"Wake up!" said the young man who had suddenly appeared by her chair. It was Nick Shapley. Nick was one of the good ones and she liked him. They had quickly become friends.

"You know, Norwood. Sharon Norwood, the one with the teenage son who's always in trouble."

She blinked at him and he grinned. "Must have been a good night," he said, raising an eyebrow.

"Now wouldn't you like to know," she said, taking a folder from the top of her in-tray and passing it to him. "Where are we on that one, by the way?"

"The son got nicked again last night and they let him cool off for a while before sending him home. No charges. He's lucky."

"Yes but she's not, is she? No money, depressed and stuck with a useless husband who won't pull his weight".

"We're doing everything we can, I promise you. I'm seeing her this week so I'll keep you posted. Thanks for this." He slapped his hand on the folder and strolled off.

Catherine leaned back in her chair and looked at her watch.

It was nearly lunchtime and she wondered what Gavin was doing. Slobbing it out in the kitchen, she decided, and eating something very unhealthy. Briefly she thought about ringing him then, rather than later. But that would be moving too fast. Sure, the sex had been amazing and they both really wanted to see each other again. Even so, it would be best to take it slow and let things happen at their own pace.

But did she really want to be hitched up to a priest? Especially one with so many unmet needs? That had been in the back of her mind since she'd first got to know him. He talked so little about his early life, she'd begun to think there was a problem there of some kind. Her work was all about people and their problems and the last thing she wanted was to have her personal life cluttered with it.

And she could see herself getting fed up with this secrecy thing. How long would she have to be the girlfriend that nobody knew about? Wasn't she worth more than that? And wouldn't he have to come out with it some time and tell people? Wouldn't they find out anyway? And then what? Marriage? Now that was really scary, she thought.

But then they did have a real friendship. She couldn't deny that. And she sensed that love was growing between them. So far it was easy and uncomplicated. They had fun and laughed at things. And when they made love, it wasn't about power games or cheap gratification. It was a genuine and simple pleasure that left them both feeling happy and secure. So what was she worried about?

When it came down to it, she thought, the whole thing could be as good or bad as they chose to make it. And somehow she knew that, whatever his faults might be, he wasn't going to be one of those pseudo-masculine types who thought women needed protecting. He would always be honest with her, she was certain of that. And she could be honest with him.

So for now she'd let it ride and see how it turned out. Tonight she would ring him. Maybe even see him. They'd talk about their day and make fun of each other. And then one of them would mention the coming weekend.

Catherine smiled to herself and looked at her watch. She thought how much she was looking forward to all that.

Chapter 7

"Hello. You must be ... "

"Stefanov Anderek" said the man, smiling warmly and extending his hand.

Gavin Salter felt relieved, as the name had momentarily gone out of his head. The man's handshake was firm and strong.

"You had no problem finding me, then."

"None at all," said the man. "And even if I had, I could have happily walked around Hadleigh Bridge all day long. It's a beautiful place."

Gavin Salter gestured ahead of them, then walked in the direction of the study.

"So this is a Church of England rectory. You guys live well." The tone was jovial and accompanied by the slight raising of one eyebrow.

Salter laughed. "It's one of the better ones, I have to admit. Take a seat. Can I get you some tea or coffee?"

"Thanks, but no", said the man, settling himself in the armchair. "I had coffee at Waterloo and I drink far too much of it anyway. And tea is a very civilised English custom, but it's not for me." And he smiled and raised the eyebrow again.

He sat with his legs crossed and the tips of his fingers loosely together. It was the relaxed attitude of a confident and self-assured person, someone who was used to being in control of things. As his eyes met the direct gaze, Salter was aware of the flustered impression he must be giving.

"Well, Father Salter, we have already spoken on the telephone and I'm now glad to meet you in person. As a matter of fact, I was staying with some old friends in Paris when I rang you. Combining business with pleasure, as I think you would say".

"Indeed" said Salter, noting the man's competent grasp of English.

"And you will recall I said I worked for the Institute for Historical and Cultural Research in Bratislava. We're located within the Slovakian Ministry of Education and Science, but in fact we're a joint initiative with the Ministry of Culture. Set up quite recently, a year or so ago. Fairly typical of European government these days. We also have links with the archaeology departments of several European universities. And, as our name suggests, we undertake research projects of an historical and cultural nature, particularly where these relate to the history of our country and our identity as a nation. Now, you must be wanting to ask me a whole load of questions, like why have I come all the way from Slovakia to see a priest? After all, we've got plenty of priests of our own I could talk to if I needed to!"

As he spoke, he unzipped the document case resting on his lap and removed some papers. But he continued to look Salter directly in the eye and his gaze did not falter.

"I kind of assumed you weren't sightseeing", said Salter, breathing slowly and trying to match the man's composure.

"No, indeed", said the man, thoughtfully stroking his heavy black moustache and looking down now at the area of floor between them, as if carefully weighing his next words before he said them.

"Father Salter", he said, resuming the eye contact. "Do you by any chance have a copy of a book entitled 'Early Christian Writings'? Or if not that one, then perhaps another book that covers the same subject matter?"

Salter was noting the handmade suit and the Rolex watch. Slovakia was not one of the wealthier post-communist countries, or so he'd heard. So how could a minor civil servant afford to kit himself out like this? And his English was impeccable. Still, he decided, that was probably his own prejudiced view of things.

"Yes, I believe I have" he said, standing up and scanning the rows of books on the shelves that lined the study walls. "Ah, there it is. Good thing I didn't chuck it out. I haven't looked at it for a few years now".

He took a small, dog-eared paperback from one of the upper shelves and blew a cloud of dust off its top edge. Then he sat down again.

"Excellent" said the man. He was looking at one of the sheets of paper. "It will be so much easier to refer to this particular book. Now, can you please find the First Letter of St Clement and turn to what I believe will be page twenty-five. And would you then read the last few lines, which, as you will note, refer to St Paul the Apostle".

Salter flicked through the pages. "Is this some sort of guessing game?" he said and frowned slightly.

"There is no guessing involved, Father Salter", said the man, putting the sheet of paper down and resting his hands on the arms of the chair. "And it certainly isn't a game. In a moment,

I will be putting to you a very important proposition. Now, if you please, would you kindly read the text I have indicated".

There was something unnerving about the way he spoke the words. He had already summed the man up as a person not to be taken lightly. Now the seriousness of his tone was close to being intimidating.

Salter started reading out loud.

"He taught righteousness to all the world; and after reaching the furthest limits of the West ... "

"The furthest limits of the West" repeated the man. Salter looked up and once again his eyes met the gaze.

"And what is the writer referring to? What exactly does he mean when he says 'furthest limits of the West'?"

Salter looked down at the words he had just read, then he looked again at the man. He felt a bit as if he were back at school, trying to cover up the fact that he hadn't done his prep.

"Well, I read something about this at theological college. It's a while back now but I seem to remember that St Clement's meaning isn't entirely clear. He could be saying that Paul made it as far as Spain. Somewhere in the Epistle to the Romans he says he's planning to go there, but I can't give you an exact quote".

"Romans chapter fifteen, verses twenty-three and twenty-four", said the man. Salter felt embarrassed at this demonstration of his own ignorance.

"Or he could mean Rome itself, which is where Paul finished his missionary journeys and eventually died".

The man nodded gently, looking down at the floor again. Then he looked up.

"There is another possibility. And that is why I have come all this way to see you". Salter noticed that the voice had suddenly become very soft.

"There is evidence to suggest that St Paul's missionary journeys took him much further even than the Iberian peninsula". He paused, and the silence in the room was almost tangible. Salter suddenly felt tense. The man continued.

"An ancient document has been discovered in my home country. The dating process is not yet complete and we have a number of experts working on it at the moment. However, it is likely that the document was written in the fourth century, perhaps even earlier. It clearly refers to a visit of St Paul and a small group of his companions to these islands, and to what you would now call Southern England. They stayed in one place for a while, perhaps a few months, and they appear during that time to have made extensive contact with the inhabitants".

Salter was sitting on the edge of the chair. Almost without realising it, he was holding his breath.

"You still haven't said how this involves me".

"The place where St Paul stayed was an ancient settlement, and it was large and important enough to enable him to meet and get to know a number of people, both residents and visitors. According to the document I mentioned, his missionary work met with a degree of success and he made several converts to the Christian Faith. There is no record of what happened to the converts or to the settlement after St Paul left. However, the document does give us some rather interesting information of another kind".

The man was fixing Salter with his eyes. And Salter found it impossible to look away.

"Apparently these new Christians made some kind of

monument to St Paul, marking his visit to their homeland. Now the document doesn't tell us exactly what sort of structure this was. But it does tell us that it was made of stones cut into a specific shape, that of a triangle, and that each one of these stones was engraved with writing or early Christian symbols. One stone, it appears, was engraved with the name 'Paul'".

The man paused, clearly allowing Gavin Salter time to take the information in. But his gaze remained fixed.

"Some time after that, the settlement came under attack and to keep them safe the stones were buried. Now according to this account, the stones remained buried. Perhaps they thought it safer to leave them where they were and they may have died before they had the chance to dig them up again. But, and this is where it involves you, Father Salter, the document gives the location of the original settlement with great precision. Apparently it became known as a holy place and even when the original settlement had been destroyed, the place itself continued to be venerated".

He paused again. Salter realised it was for effect, but he couldn't ignore the mounting excitement he was feeling.

"The ancient world was not such a primitive place as many people like to think. The references and directions this document gives enable a skilled cartographer to identify the place with a considerable degree of certainty. This has in fact been done by a team of specialists from the Institute".

The man paused again. And Salter felt a strange sensation. As if he knew what was coming next.

"There is good reason to think that the settlement was located in the place now known as Hadleigh Bridge. And because holy places have a way of keeping their identity, it is likely that the ground on which your church stands was the original site of the settlement and the monument to St Paul. To put it plainly, we believe that the stone triangles are buried somewhere in the vicinity of the church of St Mary the Virgin".

Salter let his breath out with an audible hiss. For a moment he looked down at his feet. Then he leaned back in his chair and looked across at the man.

"I don't know what to say".

"No, I don't suppose you do", said the man, smiling reassuringly. "But before you say anything at all, let me answer some of the questions which I'm sure are going through your mind. No, it's not a hoax. The Institute are not so wealthy that they can afford to send me all the way to England just to play a prank. And no, we are not mistaken, at least I don't think we are. The authenticity of the document I mentioned has been carefully researched and continues to be. So have the references which are made in it. We can't afford to get things wrong. It could mean our reputation".

"It just seems incredible", said Salter. "I mean, why should it take centuries to discover that St Paul came to this country? His other journeys are well documented. If it happened, it would be recorded somewhere, in the Acts of the Apostles or in his letters? How could no-one have known about it?"

"Yes, I see what you mean", said the man, and he stroked his moustache with one finger and looked thoughtful, as if he were weighing the arguments. "But then the New Testament writers were not historians in the sense that we understand that term. They used the information they had to suit their purpose. Maybe the story of Paul's journey to Britain was simply not relevant to the history of the Early Church. And as for the discovery taking a long time, you could say just the same about the Dead Sea Scrolls. As you know, they lay buried in the desert until the middle of the twentieth century".

Salter felt a rising frustration. He should have been able to argue with what the man was saying, at least to get the whole thing into some kind of perspective, to see it all as an interesting and plausible theory but nothing more than that. Instead he was being drawn into it. He was fascinated by this stranger from an obscure part of Europe he knew nothing about. And he was fascinated by the world of mystery and discovery which was now opening up before him. It was as if he wanted it to be true. And for once he couldn't hear the cynic inside him, who would undoubtedly have dismissed it all as a ridiculous fairytale.

"Alright" said Salter. "What you're saying kind of makes sense. I'm prepared to be open-minded about it. But tell me, what's in it for you?"

The man laughed. A deep, chesty laugh that resonated with genuine humour.

"Where do you want me to start? We are a post-communist nation. We are rediscovering our identity as a people, celebrating who we are. I'm not exaggerating, this could be one of the building blocks of the new Slovakia. What does it matter if these stones end up in the British Museum? The trail started in our country. No-one will be able to say otherwise. The credit will go to us and the Institute will be a magnet for every historian in the world".

The man rubbed the palms of his hands together, as if he were already presiding over the scenario he was describing.

"And what an opportunity for international co-operation!

What a great step forward for historical knowledge! Now that would appeal to you, wouldn't it, Father Salter?"

The man stared at him hard, and raised his eyebrows, very slightly.

"It would" said Salter, looking down at the floor and biting his lower lip reflectively. "It certainly would".

"So, you are interested?" Again the man gave him the reassuring smile.

"Well, I guess I am. Now what happens … "

Salter sat bolt upright in his chair, as a sudden realisation hit him.

"Hang on a minute! You're not expecting to dig up the churchyard, are you? I mean … I couldn't possibly … "

"My dear Father Salter" said the man, and the tone of his voice was soothing, almost compassionate. "I can assure you I had no such thing in mind. The Institute has far too much respect for ancient buildings and their environment to go about things in such a clumsy way. Our research teams have some of the finest investigative equipment in the world. We use electronic sensors to detect objects at great depths and to locate them with the highest degree of precision. Only if we were completely certain of our findings would we begin excavations, and even then it would be done only with the full approval of your authorities. I hope that goes without saying".

"Right" said Salter, and relaxed into his chair. "I suppose I should have known all that".

"I can of course understand your anxieties" said the man. "In your position I would feel exactly the same".

"So I guess you want me to start getting official permission. Obviously I would have to speak to my churchwardens and to the Parochial Church Council. And I imagine the diocese has some committee or other that needs to be informed".

"You might like to think very carefully, Father Salter, before you do any such thing". The man's voice had taken on a solemn tone. Salter found himself listening intently.

"Officialdom has a way of stamping on things before they have even seen the light of day. And that is particularly so if something challenges their narrow institutional outlook. If ecclesiastical bureaucrats took this project over, it would be a disaster. That would serve neither your interests nor mine. You and I would need to be free to work together, and to steer the project and move it forward at every stage according to our own judgement, without any outside interference and as we thought best".

The man paused, clearly making sure his words had sunk in.

"And suppose something went wrong and the project failed at an early stage. What if we couldn't find the stones? What if the worst happened and we found it had been a mistake all along? How would you look then to the people of your church and of this village, if you'd announced this great archaeological discovery and then it came to nothing?"

"So what are you suggesting?" said Salter. "I just go ahead with a research project involving my church without telling anyone? Without any kind of clearance? That's more than my job's worth. It would be highly irregular, to say the least. I'm an Anglican priest and in the Church of England things have to be done a certain way".

"I understand you perfectly" said the man. "But let us put things in their right proportion. All I am suggesting is that a small team of researchers are given access to your church and the surrounding area for a few days. Their equipment will be small, some of it handheld. They will require only the use of a single power line and their methods will be non-intrusive. I can promise you there will be no damage or disruption of any kind. And even if there were, the Institute would take full responsibility and we would regard ourselves as fully liable for whatever costs are incurred".

Again he paused, then continued.

"Why tell anyone? Except of course the congregation of your church, who can be told that a group of amateur historians or archaeologists are examining an ancient building. After all, that is not altogether a lie. You don't have to tell them who we really are and why we are here. If it so happens that we find nothing, then we leave and you will never hear from us again. But if we succeed and find what we are looking for, and I'm certain we will, then you can tell the whole world if you want to. And all the credit will go to you for being the man of faith and vision who enabled it to happen. Now how do you like that, my dear Father?"

The man leaned back luxuriously in the chair, folded his hands in his lap and smiled warmly at Salter.

Salter had been listening carefully, taking it all in, still not sure he could believe what he was hearing.

"Alright, I'm with you. We could probably do it that way. But give me some time to think about it. When do you want a decision?"

"Not for a while yet" said the man. "We are not in a hurry. Take your time. We'd like you to think about it. Then give us your decision when you are ready. And of course, we'd like you to come to Slovakia and see the document for yourself".

Salter stared at the man, wide-eyed.

"What did you say?"

The man laughed the deep, chesty laugh again.

"Well don't sound so surprised, Father Salter! Did you think we'd expect you to take our word for it? Come and see us! Be our guest! Let us show you the evidence! Believe me, it would give me and my colleagues at the Institute the greatest pleasure. Have you been to Slovakia before?"

"Never" said Salter, shaking his head in disbelief.

"Then what a wonderful opportunity it will be! You can enjoy a few days of Slovakian hospitality and then go home convinced. Of course, all your travel and accommodation expenses will be paid by the Institute".

Salter took a deep breath then let it out.

"What can I say?"

"When you have decided, contact me" said the man, and he handed him a sheet of paper with a business card stapled to it. "That's the phone number and address of my hotel in London in case you need them. But use my mobile. It'll be easier than trying to get through to a hotel. The Institute's contact details and website address are on the card. So is my secretary's email address. I thought you might want to check my identity".

The man stood up and zipped the document case.

"Thank you for giving me your time, Father Salter. It was most kind of you and it has been a great pleasure to make your acquaintance".

He walked out of the study and into the hall.

"I hope we meet again" he said, turning as he reached the door.

As they shook hands, Salter got a final impression of this authoritative, self-confident and at the same time mysterious person.

"Yes, I hope so" said Salter. Afterwards, he could not remember what his last words were.

Chapter 8

The man who now called himself Stefanov Anderek walked calmly but quickly, avoiding eye contact with the few people who passed him. He was conscious of looking like a stranger and did not want to draw attention to himself any more than he had done already.

At the station, he walked to the end of the empty platform and sat on a bench. He lit a cigarette and inhaled the smoke deeply. The next train to London was not due for another ten minutes, so he had time to relax and enjoy a smoke. He had earned it, he thought.

He finished the cigarette and stubbed it out on the platform with the sole of his shoe. Then he took out his mobile and sent a coded text message to someone somewhere in Europe, informing them that he had made contact as planned, that so far it was going well and that he would be in touch again shortly with further updates.

The train which would take him to London Waterloo drew into Hadleigh Bridge and he got on. As it pulled out, he read through the printout of an email giving confirmation of his hotel reservation. He expected it to be a non-descript sort of place. A room the size of a wardrobe and nowhere you could get a decent meal. Typical of London. Still, it was good cover if anyone started looking for a trail. And they would. After an operation like this one, they would be looking for a long time.

He took out the loose-leaf notebook again. He would need to check the names of the stations, just to be sure he had them all.

. . .

Gavin Salter stood by the window of his study, absent-mindedly flicking the pages of the paperback called Early Christian Writings and thinking about what he had just heard.

Of course the man had been right. He would have to keep the whole thing quiet. If he even mentioned it to the Archdeacon or the Bishop, he would immediately find himself tangled up in the whole machinery of ecclesiastical bureaucracy. There would be procedures and meetings to go to, and long delays while committees made their minds up. If indeed they ever did. It could even be taken out of his hands altogether. And if these Slovakian guys found themselves dealing with a load of stuffed shirts, they could decide they'd had enough of it big time and pull out. And then a fantastic opportunity would be lost.

He slid the book back into the space it had left on the shelves. Then he went into the kitchen, got another cold beer from the fridge and sat down again in his study chair.

Why did he feel himself being drawn into this? What did he think he was going to get out of it? Maybe it was the pull of the unknown. The sense of adventure this thing seemed to have about it. After all, this could be a chance to improve his life.

Not that there was too much wrong with the life he had. But he had never imagined himself being a country priest for ever, and he couldn't take it for granted that the Church of England would always be able to satisfy his career aspirations. He had heard of too many priests who had got stuck on the lower rungs of the promotion ladder and gone to seed in a back-end-of-nowhere parish. This could mean a consultant's job working for European government agencies, or running educational tours for a holiday company. Or even some kind of overseas chaplaincy. Why not? The possibility was there, staring him in the face. All he needed to do was take what was being offered.

He would ring the man tonight. Of course, he could always sleep on it and think about it again tomorrow before making a final decision. But why delay things? He had to admit to himself he'd already made the decision and he was pretty sure it was the right one. Now where was that sheet of paper and that business card the man had given him?

The phone rang.

"Afternoon vicar" said Catherine.

"Oh ... er ... hello Catherine. Good to hear from you. I wasn't expecting you till this evening."

There was a brief silence.

"Have you got someone with you?" she said.

"Er ... no ... why?"

"It's just that you sound a bit jumpy. And 'Catherine' sounds very formal. You usually say 'darling', especially if we're ... well, never mind. Anyway, things are a bit quiet here and I was getting bored, so I thought I'd call you."

She giggled softly.

"Sorry, I didn't mean I was calling you 'cos I was bored.

That sounds really awful. What I really meant was I couldn't wait another minute to hear the seductive tones of your voice and feel your hot breath down the mouthpiece. So what about tonight?"

Salter felt himself about to stammer, so he took a deep breath.

"No, I'm afraid I can't do anything tonight. I've got a lot of phone calls to make and it'll probably take most of the evening. And then I've got that sermon to finish. I really need to get down to it".

"Oh. I see". She hoped she didn't sound disappointed. She had never believed in using emotional pressure to get her own way.

"So maybe later in the week? Do you want to give me a call when you're not so busy?"

"Great" he said. "I'll do that." At another time, he might have registered the fact that she was giving him space and not tying him down. And he would have been grateful for that. But now he was too distracted to notice her consideration for him.

They rang off. And as he put the phone down, he realised he'd just told her a lie. The first one he had ever told her. He didn't have a lot of phone calls to make that evening. Only one. And he wasn't thinking about the sermon.

...

Something wasn't right, thought Catherine. Something had changed. Something had come between them. Something. Even over the phone she could sense it.

Maybe he'd gone off her already. It was a bit early for that, they'd only just started. But it could have happened. After all, he was a self-confessed womaniser and he'd at least had the decency to tell her that before things got too heavy. He'd probably met somebody else he fancied more. He could even be with her right now. Maybe he'd been doing that all the time. So much for him being honest with her.

She picked up a typed sheet of paper from her desk and without thinking screwed it into a tight ball. Then she threw it with some force into the wastepaper bin next to her, wondering too late if it had been anything important.

Why the hell should she care anyway? She'd made the mistake of getting involved with some wally in a cassock with an over-inflated ego and a load of emotional baggage who thought he was literally God's gift to women. Now it was all over and really she ought to be pleased. He'd never get the chance to mess her about and make use of her. She'd never find herself slotted into his social calendar to suit his convenience. She'd never have to listen to his transparent excuses as to why he couldn't see her that evening or go away with her that weekend. She'd had a narrow escape and she was grateful for it and that was that.

But it wasn't and she knew it. She stood up and walked over to the office kitchen. Thinking she couldn't stomach any more coffee, she made a cup of herbal tea and stirred it slowly as she looked out through the window of the Social Services building at the car park below.

She was over-reacting, and that wasn't like her. All he had done so far was to make some weak excuse for not seeing her tonight. And why did she think it was a lie? He could just as easily have been telling the truth. He had his work to do the same as she did and that was his business. It was not her style to delve into every detail of someone else's life. Control was not what she was about. In any case, when she rang him again, things would probably be right back on track. They would see each other at the weekend and she'd soon find they had the same easy-going relationship with a bit of sex thrown in.

She sipped the herbal tea, briefly thinking how vile it tasted. Looking back on it, she was surprised at her reaction. Her feelings for him clearly ran deeper than she'd realised. Faced with the possibility of the whole thing falling apart, she had come close to panic. And that worried her. Could she really afford to feel that way about someone?

She decided the tea was more than she could take and threw it down the sink. Then she walked back to her desk.

Now where was her diary? She just needed to check what was happening at the weekend. And think about what they might get up to.

Chapter 9

"So, you have decided to go ahead. Somehow I thought you would" said the voice of the man who called himself Stefanov Anderek.

Gavin Salter was sitting in front of the computer in his study, looking at the homepage of the Institute's website. Earlier he had emailed the address shown on the man's business card and shortly afterwards had received a cheerful reply from the woman who was his secretary, confirming that he was the Institute's Programme Director, as the card said. He'd also checked out the websites of a few Slovakian government ministries and the telephone numbers and email addresses seemed to line up with the ones on the card. Everything seemed perfectly in order.

"Yes indeed" said Salter. "It all sounds too good to miss".

"Wonderful" said the man. "You won't regret this, I can assure you. And the Institute will have every reason to be grateful to you for your kind assistance. Now, how are we going to proceed? Are we agreed on a certain level of confidentiality? Or shall we say, restricted information? Sounds better, don't you think?" The man chuckled.

"I'm going to tell the churchwardens and one or two of the people who look after the place. I'll say they're amateurs, as you suggested. I might even invent a local history society from the next town, or something like that. And I'll suggest they keep it to themselves because we don't want anyone sticking their noses into what goes on at the church. They'll go for that one alright".

The man chuckled again. "Sounds like you have it all sewn up, Father Salter. I look forward to working with you very much. And like I said, it will all be over in a few days".

"So what if you find what you're looking for?"

"Well, I certainly hope that will be the case" said the man.

"As I told you when we met, we are pretty confident that we're looking in the right place. And when we find what we're after ... well, that's almost another project. There'll be a lot more work involved then, and you of course will take a large chunk of the credit for it all".

"That's what I like to hear" said Salter. "Now what else do I need to do at this end of things? How many of these guys will there be? And where will they be staying? I guess they'll need to be on top of their work".

"How many of them there will be I'm not sure yet. Now that I have the go-ahead from you, I will be meeting with colleagues back at the Institute and we will get to work on putting a team together. We will be arranging accommodation for them nearby and they will have arranged their own transport, so there will be nothing for you to do. It's all down to us. However, there is one matter on which I would greatly appreciate your co-operation".

"Sure, if I can help".

"Our researchers will need some kind of indoor work area. It doesn't have to be very large. Somewhere they can use a laptop and make a few notes and diagrams. And if possible make tea and coffee during their meal breaks. Is there anywhere like that in the vicinity?"

"No problem" said Salter. "The church has a small room built onto it. You can get to it from the church but it's got its own outside door as well. It's a kind of social area. Tiny kitchen, foldaway chairs and tables, that sort of thing. And its own lavatory, which comes in handy. It gets used on Sundays after the service and occasionally by a pensioners' group on Thursday afternoons, but apart from that it's free. I could probably give your blokes the key".

"Father Salter, you are a miracle-worker! I can't thank you enough." The man's voice was brimming with gratitude. "This is all falling nicely into place. Now all that remains is to fix up your trip to my homeland. You can of course stay with us as long as you wish, but my guess is you won't want to be away from your parish too long. I'm due back at the Institute the day after tomorrow, so just ring me in the next twenty-four hours and let me have some dates. Then I will make the necessary arrangements and all your travel details will be sent to you. I look forward to showing you Slovakia".

The man switched his mobile off, slipped it back into the pocket of his jacket and lit a Marlboro. Standing on the small balcony of his third floor room, he looked down at the street below.

He had known all along about the room built onto the church. It was one of the reasons they had chosen St Mary's Church.

Chapter 10

Holy Communion at seven a.m. on Saturdays was a longstanding tradition at St Peter's, Wimhurst. The other two churches had never felt the need for an act of worship at such an ungodly hour, clearly believing that their Saturday morning lie-in was infinitely more sacred than anything likely to happen in church. As he leaned against the kitchen sink unit, yawning and rubbing his eyes, Gavin Salter was inclined to agree with them. Still, he thought, he was a priest and celebrating the Eucharist was what he was all about, so he shouldn't really complain. And anyway, he'd done it now and his time was his own. He filled the kettle and switched it on.

It was eight o'clock. The roads had been empty, as they usually were at that hour, so the journey by car had taken him about five minutes each way. He had spoken to Catherine on Thursday and she had suggested coming round to the vicarage at about eleven. Since then he had worked out what he was going to tell her. He hoped she would believe it and not think he was just covering up the fact that he was seeing someone else.

But then, he wondered, did he really care whether she believed him or not? Okay, he'd started getting really fond of her. Perhaps he even loved her. But she was just another woman and one day it would all be over. Just like it always was. Just like it had been with the others. He knew it would be. And so what if it left him with a bad conscience? He'd survive that. He'd done it before. And in any case, he certainly wasn't going to waste an opportunity like this for the sake of an affair. His involvement with her could get in the way and might even ruin everything. In some ways, it might be better if it ended now.

On Wednesday, he had rung Anderek again and agreed dates for the trip. The Institute would fly him over business class the following Monday, then Anderek would meet him at Bratislava Airport. The rest of the itinerary was still a bit vague, but Anderek had done his now familiar laugh and had promised him it would all be very interesting and that he would not regret it. By Saturday he would be home.

An old friend of his from years back, Bill Hoxton, who had helped him out before, had agreed to cover the weekday services and pick up on any urgent parish business. And clearing it with the Archdeacon had been no problem. Salter had turned up for his recent annual interview with a massive hangover and the Archdeacon had immediately concluded he was suffering the effects of stress due to overwork and recommended he take a few days off as soon as he could arrange it. Up until then, Salter had always regarded these annual interviews as a complete and utter waste of time.

So his line would be: away for a few days, short break, need the rest, back in time for Sunday. That would do for the churchwardens and anyone else who was at all interested in what he did. He suddenly felt the cynic in him coming out and he wondered why.

The kettle was boiling vigorously. He put two spoons of dark instant coffee into a mug and poured the water. He'd better start thinking about packing. That was always a pain in the arse, he thought smiling to himself. Whatever the trip, the suitcase was never big enough. He'd need clericals, which would mean his decent black suit and black shoes, and a couple of shirts. And he mustn't forget to pack the collars. Then something smart-casual for eating out. He was sure he'd be doing that a few times. He would travel in jeans and his favourite old Timberland boat shoes, and a coat, probably his leather one. He'd be comfortable on the plane and the outfit would do for sightseeing as well. Socks, underwear, the paperback he'd started last week. Lightweight sweater, just in case ...

The doorbell rang.

Now who the hell was that? Couldn't he get just a few minutes to himself without someone pestering him? Calm down, he thought, it could be the post. He opened the door.

Catherine Laurence stood on the doorstep. She wore a loose cotton dress and her feet were bare.

"Couldn't wait till eleven" she said, her voice soft and slightly husky.

Salter grabbed her arm and pulled her inside. Then he looked up and down the road outside before closing the door.

"It's a bloody good thing there's no-one about" he said irritably. "You know what this neighbourhood is ... "

He just had time to notice that the cotton dress was lying on the hall floor in a crumpled heap and that she was completely naked before she threw her arms around his neck and clamped her wide-open mouth onto his. He held her, responding to the passionate kiss. Then he pulled away from her.

"What are you doing?"

"I think sex is the word for it" she said, slipping his clerical collar off and starting to unbutton his shirt. He grasped her hand.

"Listen, Catherine, I've got work to do".

"Never mind work" she said and kissed him again. "You can do me instead. Much better for you". And letting go of him she darted towards the stairs and bounded up to the landing.

"See you in the bedroom!" she called over the banisters.

He sighed resignedly and walked up the stairs to the main bedroom. He stopped in the doorway.

He had been about to say something. Something about how he had things to get on with and how important they all were and how annoyed he was going to be if she got under his feet just as he was trying to get them done. But now he had forgotten that completely.

The bedding had been thrown onto the floor. Catherine was lying face down on the bed, her head resting on one arm, her body silhouetted against the dark blue of the undersheet, her legs apart. His eye followed the cleft of her buttocks down to the tuft of hair at the opening of her vagina and, as he looked at her, he was suddenly aware of every curve of her flesh and every fold of her skin. And he was imagining every scent and every taste of every part of her.

He undressed and stretched out on the bed beside her. He kissed her shoulder, softly and tenderly, then placed the tip of his finger on the back of her neck and slowly ran it down her spine. For a brief moment she was still, with no movement but the rise and fall of her breathing. Then she rolled onto her side and pulled him against her, once again pressing her lips against his. He felt himself giving way, as if every impulse within him was releasing itself, and their tongues explored the recesses of each others mouth with a hungry passion.

He pushed her roughly onto her back, biting into her neck and digging his fingernails into her shoulder blades. She groaned and her legs closed around him. He entered her, slowly at first, as he luxuriated in her warm moisture. Then he thrust into her. She climaxed, crying out as the orgasm racked her body, and he held his hand gently over her mouth to muffle the sound. Then he came, shuddering uncontrollably, until finally the storm was past and he collapsed on top of her, his face buried in her hair.

They lay there, drenched in sweat, for what seemed like hours.

"Cover us up. It's cold" she said in a croaking voice.

He reached down with one arm and pulled the duvet over them. Then they fell asleep.

. . .

They showered together and got dressed and he made coffee and toast and scrambled some eggs. They sat at the table in the kitchen.

"Tell me about it" she said, peering at him over her coffee mug.

Salter looked genuinely surprised.

"Tell you about what?"

"Whatever it is you've got on your mind". And she reached across the table and took hold of his hand. "Look, the last thing

I want to be is the nosey woman in your life. But you know I care about you and I get the feeling ... well, you know ... that something's worrying you".

He looked at her without speaking. This is it, he thought. Better make it sound convincing.

"I've got to be away for a few days next week".

"Oh, is that all?" She visibly relaxed and smiled her broad smile. "I thought you'd had some bad news or something. So where are you off to? Anywhere nice?"

"Well I suppose it is bad news, really. Someone in my family has just died. She was very old, so it's not a tragic death. But the relatives have already started arguing about the will and threatening to get solicitors in and there's no-one who can sort her affairs out because none of them trust each other. So, as the priest in the family, I've been called in to mediate and try and make some sense out of it. And if I don't go, I'll always feel I've let them down. So there you are".

She had been listening intently. Now she bit her lower lip and nodded slowly.

"I'm with you. They're really difficult, these family things. And I can understand the way you feel about it. It must be putting a lot of pressure on you".

For a moment they sat in silence, still holding hands.

"Do you have far to go?" she said.

"Oh, it's .. er ... just outside Newcastle. I'm getting a train Monday morning".

Catherine looked at him thoughtfully. Then she looked down at the table.

"So you've got relatives up north? Didn't you make a joke once about your family all being snooty southerners?"

Sod it, he thought. I've messed things up.

"Sure, most of them are" he said, trying to hold on to his composure. "But there's a branch of the family up north. I've never had much to do with them. I guess I tend to forget about them. You know how it is".

"Mmm." Catherine looked down at the table again. There was another silence.

"But they obviously feel close enough to you to call on you at a time like this. And they must trust you if they're asking you to sort all this out. Even if they don't trust each other". She didn't look up as she spoke.

Salter took a deep breath.

"Yes. Of course. You're absolutely right. I guess they must do".

His fabricated story now had several cracks in it and they were big enough to see right through. And he was painfully aware of it. This time the silence was much longer.

"So I guess I shouldn't expect to hear from you for a while, if you've got all that stuff to handle" she said.

"No, I guess not" he said, hoping that the guilt he now felt wasn't showing on his face. "I can't say exactly where I'll be or what I'll be doing. And I'll probably need to keep the mobile switched off if I'm into heavy conversations. When I get back on Saturday, I'll give you a call. That's a promise".

"Fine" said Catherine, and smiled again. "I'll be waiting. Now let me wash up".

"That's alright" he said, standing up purposefully. "I've got to tidy up in here, so I'll do the lot together. I expect you need to get off".

"Yes, I'm sure I can find something to do" she said, and the disappointment in her voice was slight but unmistakeable.

"Thanks for breakfast" she said as she hugged him and kissed him on the cheek. Then she put her hand into the pocket of her dress and took out a bunch of keys.

"My car's parked down the road. Sorry about the dramatic entry. I'll be very discreet leaving".

She turned away and walked into the hall, opened the front door and closed it behind her.

Standing alone in the kitchen, Salter felt he should have said something more. But he knew he had nothing more to say. At least nothing that was worth saying.

Chapter 11

THE BELL WAS RINGING FOR the Parish Eucharist at St Mary's. Catherine listened to it as she lay in bed and looked at the sky through the bedroom window of her flat.

So that's it, she thought. It would have to end now. It couldn't go on. She wouldn't ever be able to trust him. He'd told her a pack of lies and hadn't even bothered to make it sound convincing. It was a shabby thing for him to have done. She was worth a lot more than that. When he got back from this spurious trip of his, she'd have a few things to say to him.

She felt oddly detached from her own feelings, as if she were observing herself from the outside. She was angry, no doubt about that. The anger had been growing since yesterday. She was angry at being taken in. Angry that he'd manipulated her into being the obedient little girl whose only purpose in life was to be there for him and to massage his already over-inflated ego whenever he wanted her to. Why hadn't she seen the warning signs?

But at another level she couldn't make sense of it. Something wasn't right. It shouldn't be ending this way. What had happened between them had promised so much. The whole thing was like a jigsaw with a piece missing. More than anything else, she felt confused.

Maybe this wasn't the time to make final decisions, she thought. She wasn't the kind of person who acted in anger. In a tense situation she usually managed to stand back until she'd cooled down. She would certainly have to confront him. There was no way he was going to get away with feeding her a load of crap. But wasn't there some possibility of salvaging the whole thing? Perhaps if he was completely honest with her from now on. Then it might be worth trying one more time.

But then how would she know if he was being honest or not? How could she possibly know after the way he'd behaved? Why was she setting herself up to be conned all over again? "Don't even think about it!" she said out loud.

She kicked the duvet off her naked body, stretched her arms and legs and rolled out of bed. Then, shaking her hair like a mane, she walked across the room and stood in front of the full-length mirror.

She cupped her hands under her breasts and lifted them slightly, stroking her nipples with the tips of her fingers. Then she slapped her stomach with both hands, briefly holding it in then letting it out again. Could do with losing an inch or two there, she thought. But then, why bother? She'd always liked the way she looked. Not in a narcissistic kind of way, but because she'd always thought that feeling good about herself was important. Self-confidence and self-esteem mattered to her more than anything else. She'd never been interested in conforming to some glossy magazine stereotype. That was a one-way ticket to depression and anorexia and in her line of work she'd seen the results of it too often.

She went into the flat's tiny kitchen, made a mug of tea and took it back to bed with her. Then wrapping the duvet closely around her and snuggling into the pillows, she thought about the day ahead.

Her first thought was what she might have done if she'd been seeing him today. But that isn't going to happen, she said to herself. So forget it. And she pushed the thought out of her mind.

What she really fancied was brunch at that pub she'd been to the other day. The food was good there and there was plenty of it. So it would be a bloody mary, or maybe two, followed by a club sandwich. She could ring up some of the crowd from work. They'd been nagging her to get together for a while now. Jennifer maybe. And Richard. And Maggie, of course. She got on really well with her. If none of them had any plans, they might be up for drinks and a bit of chat. Then afterwards they could come back to her place for a couple of hours. And it might turn into supper and a few glasses of wine. Yes, she liked the idea of all that.

In the bathroom, she turned the shower on, testing the temperature with her bare foot, and for the next ten minutes luxuriated as the hot water cascaded over her body. Back in the bedroom, she took time choosing her underwear, finally settling on deep red satin knickers and a matching bra that lifted her breasts into a sensuous cleavage. She might get lucky, she thought to herself and smiled.

She pulled on a tight-fitting black sweater with a low V-neck, then struggled into a pair of white cotton slacks. Had they shrunk in the wash or had she put on weight? she wondered as she held her breath and buttoned the waistband. Then she pushed the sleeves of the sweater up and put a heavy silver bracelet on her left arm. Slipping her feet into gold stiletto-heeled sandals, she looked at herself in the mirror. Yes, she thought. That was good. That was how she wanted to look.

Suddenly she realised she was thinking about him again and imagining the comments he'd make about her outfit and the way she looked. Angrily, she stomped across the room and sat on the edge of the bed. What the hell was going on? What was all this about? Surely she wasn't pining for the useless bastard! Did she really want him to walk through the door and sweep her off her feet with a few more of his carefully-fabricated stories? For all she knew she could meet someone else this week. Even today. Someone who'd be more than just a waste-of-time. Someone she could trust. Someone who wasn't just looking to add to his list of conquests.

But in spite of herself, images of the hours they'd spent together were flashing through her mind. The passionate sex. His body against hers. His hands gently caressing her. The long conversations and the things he'd told her about himself. The laughter. And the moments when they'd said nothing, but just held each other, happy to be there and to be together.

So what was it she wanted?

And then she knew what it was she wanted. She wanted him to be a different person. She wanted him to be the person she'd begun to love and care about. Not one who was so afraid of commitment that he had to run away and hide behind a barrier of pretence.

And wasn't that the worst kind of fantasy and self-delusion? He wasn't going to be a different person. Why should he be? She'd discovered early on who he was and what he was really like and she ought to be grateful for that. At least she'd never be hurt by him. Well, no more than she had been already.

She stood up and walked over to the wardrobe, and took a black three-quarter length cashmere coat off its hanger. She hoped she wouldn't be too warm in it. The weather forecast had promised a mild day. Let's go for it, she thought and pressed the on-button on her mobile. Now did she have Jennifer's number?

Without meaning to, she was thinking about him again. And what she would say to him when he got back.

Chapter 12

Gavin Salter slung his leather coat over one arm and wheeled his suitcase through the nothing-to-declare exit. Service on the five-hour flight via Prague had been good and he was still savouring the lunch and the champagne cognac that had rounded it off. It was the first time he had flown business class and he was thinking he ought to find an excuse for doing it again some time, especially if someone else was paying. One of the customs officers eyed him critically and for a moment he wondered if he was going to be stopped, but then the man looked away. It was a bureaucrat's job to glare at people, he thought, and this guy was only doing his job. He walked into the arrivals hall where a crowd of people were standing behind the barrier, some of them holding up notices with names written on.

"Father Salter" said a loud voice he recognised.

Stefanov Anderek was standing at the far end of the barrier. He was wearing a black jacket, white linen shirt open at the neck, tan slacks and brown suede casuals. The expensive outfit singled him out from the crowd and Salter spotted him immediately. They shook hands and once again Salter noticed the firm, strong handshake.

"So, how was the flight? I hope they looked after you. The airline will be hearing from me if they didn't!"

Anderek laughed and slapped him gently on the shoulder, gesturing in the direction they were going to walk. There was a genuine warmth and friendliness in his voice and all Salter's anxieties about this trip into the unknown began to dissipate. Even the guilt he had felt about lying to Catherine was slowly disappearing.

"It was very good, Mr Anderek ... "

"Please! call me Stefanov!" he interrupted. "I know all about you English. You love formality!"

They carried on walking and Salter looked around the arrivals hall. It was teeming with people and announcements in different languages crackled over the public address system. The whole atmosphere was one of life and movement and he suddenly felt exhilarated. Ever since he was a child, he had loved airports and the feeling of going somewhere.

"We're not too far from the city centre" said Anderek. "I think it's about ten kilometres. It shouldn't take more than half an hour if the traffic's good. You're booked into the Carmen and I can promise you a very comfortable stay there".

They walked out of the airport into a moderately cold, clear day. The sky was bright blue with just a few clouds. The air was crisp and bracing.

"That's our car, over there" said Anderek, pointing to a large silver-grey BMW parked a few yards away. "The driver's name is Yanik. He's one of the Institute staff and he's doing me a favour today. The Institute doesn't have a budget for chauffeurs". He said this with a smile and a sideways glance.

Yanik stepped forward. "Welcome to Slovakia" he said,

putting Salter's case and leather coat into the car's spacious boot and avoiding eye contact. His accent was thick and he spoke the words slowly. Salter guessed he didn't know much English. He was aged about thirty. He wasn't tall, but he had the build of a rugby player. His hands were massive. The pale blue eyes were deep set and his blonde hair was cut short, although it grew thickly down the back of his neck. His nose was flat and misshapen, as if it had at some time been broken with considerable force. There was a small, gold ring in his left ear. Salter's immediate thought was that he looked a thug, but he decided that was prejudice and dismissed it from his mind.

Anderek held the rear door open and Salter climbed in, noticing the smell of new leather and cigarette tobacco. The seat was luxuriously comfortable and at once he relaxed. Anderek got in beside him and the car glided off.

"Well, Father Salter, we have a lot to talk about and some important plans to make. Assuming of course that we succeed in convincing you and that you wish to proceed".

"I'm here to be convinced" said Salter, "and you've already made a very good case".

"I can assure you, I'm going to make an even better case" said Anderek. "But for now, enjoy your first day with us. And please don't judge our country by the roads into the capital. Tomorrow you will see some of the most beautiful scenery Slovakia has to offer".

They sat in silence as the car pulled away from the airport and Salter got his first glimpse of the outskirts of Bratislava through the car window. It was something like what he had expected. Square and uninteresting buildings, pavements in need of repair, the occasional colourless advertisement hoarding. He could see why Anderek didn't want him to make any judgements. Still, he thought, the city centre was bound to be an improvement, at least from what he'd read in the guide book he'd bought at Heathrow. And in any case, he wasn't in the mood for doing an analysis of post-communist societies. He was here to enjoy himself.

He looked at his watch and wondered what Catherine was doing. When he got back he would sort things out with her. They'd had some good times and he was very fond of her. He couldn't deny that. He'd have to try and find a convincing explanation for the lie he'd told her. But then if things all went to plan, he wouldn't have to. Of course he couldn't have told her where he was going or why, any more than he could have told the people at church. It had to be a secret. When it all came together, she'd understand and she'd forget all about it and forgive him for lying to her. She might even be impressed that he'd pulled off something this big. He could just see her dying to come with him on his next trip out here. And maybe she could. If she didn't get in the way.

"Here we are, my dear Father" said Anderek's voice, and Salter snapped out of his thoughts. The car slowed down and came to a halt in what was clearly the old part of the city. He opened the door and stepped out onto a smooth pavement and looked up at the enormous building in front of him.

"The Hotel Carmen" said Anderek, with a clear note of pride in his voice. "It's one of the best in Bratislava. You're booked in here for five nights".

Yanik put the suitcase down on the pavement next to him. Salter noticed that once again he was avoiding eye contact.

"Shall we say seven-thirty for dinner? I'll meet you at

reception" said Anderek, and he placed his hand on Salter's shoulder in a gesture full of warmth and friendship. "It's really good to see you here. I'm looking forward very much to the next few days".

Anderek got into the front seat next to Yanik and the car pulled slowly away and disappeared down a narrow street.

Gavin Salter looked up again at the tall, imposing building that was the Hotel Carmen. He counted seven storeys. The ground floor was skirted by massive columns and it fronted onto a wide, tree-lined pedestrian area laid with grey cobble stones. This was some place to stay, he thought. A lot better than he was used to on his stipend.

He wheeled his suitcase through the main entrance door, stopping briefly to look around the spacious reception. The old-fashioned elegance was straight out of an episode of Poirot and he smiled to himself as he thought of the famous detective gliding across the black-and-white tiled floor and sitting down in one of the enormous armchairs to read *Le Monde*. That was just the sort of thing he and Catherine would enjoy watching, curled up on the sofa in the rectory with a bottle of red wine and a large bag of those expensive sea-salt crisps that she liked.

For God's sake, why was he thinking about her again? He was here to relax and have a good time and she was a long way away.

"Can I help you, sir?"

The young man was standing behind the reception desk. Salter walked over to him, suddenly feeling slightly nervous.

"Er ... my name is ... er ... Salter, and I've just ... "

"Yes, of course Father Salter. We've been expecting you and your room is ready. I do hope you will have a pleasant stay with us. Now if I could please have your passport and ask you to complete this form".

Salter handed over the passport, noting the young man's confidence and easy command of English. He took a pen from its elegant holder on the desk and wrote the required details on the form.

"Thank you, Father Salter" said the young man and with a barely perceptible gesture of his forefinger summoned a porter to stand expectantly at Salter's side. "I'm sure you will find your room most comfortable, but please do not hesitate to let us know if there is anything you need".

He placed a key on the polished surface of the desk and the porter picked it up.

"If you would follow me please, sir" said the porter, and taking the suitcase he led the way in the direction of the lift.

The room was on the third floor and as he followed the porter down the thickly carpeted corridor, Salter hoped the view would be something more interesting than the back door of the hotel kitchen. They arrived at the room and the porter unlocked the door and stood back to allow Salter to go in. Then he followed him and placed the suitcase flat onto a luggage cradle that stood just inside the door. Meanwhile Salter had reached into his jeans pocket for the collection of notes and coins he had strategically placed there and tipped the man fifty koruna, hoping that would not be too little, or too much.

"Thank you, sir" said the porter mechanically and left the room, closing the door quietly behind him. Salter went over to the window and pushed back the net curtains, and was immediately pleased with what he saw. The grey, white and cream-coloured buildings of the old town with their red roofs stretched ahead of him and below was the pedestrian area at the front of the building. He looked at his watch and it said three fifty-five. Remembering he had not yet adjusted it for European time, he put it forward an hour.

He turned back into the room. There wouldn't be much to complain about here, he thought, even for a fussy bastard like him. In fact, it was everything he could have hoped for. It was spacious and richly furnished, and gold brocade curtains hung to the floor from both windows. The furniture was classical in style but clearly new. A writing desk with a heavy brass reading lamp stood against one wall and the two upholstered chairs were tastefully satin-striped. He investigated the bathroom and as he opened the door and switched the light on, a powerful extractor whirred into life. It was predictably small, but the bath and shower would allow room for manoeuvre, he decided, and feeling the towels he noted they were luxuriously soft.

He removed his leather coat and threw it over one of the chairs, lay on the bed and kicked off his Timberlands. Well, this could be a life-changing moment, he thought. Then he laughed to himself, realising the phrase sounded like something off one of those management training courses. But he was beginning to feel he'd definitely done the right thing by agreeing to all this. It was a real adventure, the sort of thing that didn't come along too often. The sort of thing you couldn't afford to miss when it did. He was going to enjoy being pampered for a few days. And then? Well, he couldn't be sure at this stage. From what Anderek had said, all kinds of good things could come out of it. Probably best not to have too many expectations. Just go with it and let it happen.

He wondered again why Anderek had been so vague about their itinerary. Then he decided the man was probably being ultra careful. It was his project and he didn't want word of it getting out to anyone else in case they stole his thunder. That made sense.

Then a thought crossed his mind and for a moment it disturbed him. For academics, these people seemed to have an awful lot of money. Okay, so they had volunteer chauffeurs. But business-class flights? Top hotels? Luxury cars? Not to mention all this expensive investigative equipment Anderek had talked about at their first meeting. Some educational institutions were struggling to keep afloat, especially in the post-communist world. And Slovakia was always reckoned to have got the bad end of the deal when they split with the Czech Republic. Their government wouldn't have any cash to throw around. And this Institute for Historical and Cultural Research, or whatever it was called, wasn't even a long established body. According to what Anderek had told him, it was an inter-departmental initiative, the kind of thing which would have restricted funding in the first place and which would constantly have to justify what funds it had.

Why hadn't he thought of this before? Perhaps he had. Perhaps he had preferred not to ask himself the question.

No, he thought. This was not his problem. There could be any number of reasons why the outfit was flushed with money. They could have wealthy backers. There were plenty of millionaires around who'd got themselves *nouveau riche* on the sale of the old state assets. That was well known. One or two of them could have decided to bankroll this whole operation. Maybe they had a stake in doing so. Mother country and all that. So he'd leave that one and not worry about it. Especially if he was currently reaping the benefits of it. And he had begun to think Anderek was a good sort of chap. One he could trust.

He yawned and realised he felt tired. His eyes closed. This bed's really comfortable, he thought as he drifted into a shallow sleep.

As he slept, a dream took shape in his mind, a confused dream in which the scenes switched from one to another at rapid speed. He stood in a dark room, the walls covered in large pictures, and in the gloom he could only just see the outline of their frames. Anderek was there. And Yanik. Except that Yanik, who had been average height, was now enormous, towering over both of them. And the gold ring in his ear had become the size of a dinner plate. Anderek and Yanik turned and walked quickly through a door and out of the room. Gavin Salter tried to follow them, and then the room suddenly became St Mary's Church. It too was dark. Much darker than he had ever known it. The church was empty, except for one person standing there. It was Catherine. He sensed she couldn't see him and he tried as hard as he could to shout to her, but no sound came from his throat. Then the building changed again. This time it was an airport and it was broad daylight, but the whole building was empty. There was not a person in sight. Through the windows he could see the runways, but there were no aircraft on them. Then suddenly he was running through the airport's empty halls, chasing something but not knowing what it was.

He was awake. There was a light sweat on his forehead. For a moment he lay there trying to make sense of the dream, but it was already fading. He wiped the sweat from his forehead with his hand and looked at his watch. It was nearly six thirty. He rolled off the bed. The dream was gone now and he wondered how long he had slept.

He unpacked his suitcase and hung the clothes in the wardrobe. Then he brushed his teeth, undressed and showered. He stood for a long time under the shower, stretching his limbs and running the water alternately hot and cold, and he washed his hair with a good-quality shampoo he found on the bathroom shelf along with various other toiletries provided by the hotel. Feeling refreshed and invigorated, he dried himself with a large thick fluffy towel, applied deodorant to his underarms and splashed his face and neck with cologne.

He always liked to have a choice of things to wear when he travelled and the suitcase he had brought was quite large and held several of his favourite items of clothing. Opening the wardrobe, he surveyed the various garments, finally settling on a light grey jacket with a discreet check and a pair of black cotton chinos. To these he added a dark blue button-down shirt and black lace-up shoes. Examining himself in the full-length mirror, he decided he was satisfied and looked at his watch again. Just time for a drink before Anderek arrived. He picked up his wallet, switched his mobile on and put his passport into the inside pocket of his jacket. Then shutting the door of the room, he turned the key, checked it was locked and walked to the lift.

The subdued lighting in the hotel bar combined perfectly with the dark wood and leather upholstery to create an atmosphere of comfort and cosiness. He felt he could easily have stayed there all evening without setting a foot outside. At the bar, he spent some time pondering the selection of drinks on offer and eventually accepted the barman's recommendation, a large glass of the chilled sparkling white wine which was apparently a favourite in that part of Slovakia. After giving the barman his room number, he sat down in a corner seat.

The bar was almost empty and he guessed most of the residents had abandoned the hotel at this hour in favour of the winding streets of the old town. A business-man type was sitting on a bar stool drinking beer and reading a newspaper, his leather briefcase on the floor beside him. On the other side of the room, a middle-aged man and woman sat over elaborate cocktails and the occasional word of German drifted over in his direction.

At times like this, he was glad he was a solitary kind of person. Large cities like this one could be the loneliest places on Earth. He reckoned he understood what loneliness was. It wasn't an emotion like everyone thought it was. It was more like a drug. It could slowly destroy people, unless they were like him and had built up a tolerance to it. His solitary nature had more than once been his salvation, especially when he was young. And since he'd been a priest with "the cure of souls" as they called it, his liking for his own company had proved to be very useful on occasions. He'd always found the priesthood to be a lonely thing. It was difficult to share it with anyone. A lot of the time it was just him and God. And God didn't take the loneliness away so that it would never be a problem again. God didn't do things that way. That wasn't how God worked. So being alone with God sometimes felt like the ultimate loneliness. And that was alright. He could handle it. Well, most of the time.

He'd been sipping his wine slowly and almost without realising it running the tip of his finger round the rim of a large ashtray on the table in front of him. The wine was good. He must have a few more of those before going back to England, he thought as he drained the glass.

Chapter 13

Anderek had arrived exactly on time as Salter sat in reception waiting for him. They left the hotel and walked down one of the streets off the pedestrian area.

"This is one of my favourite places to eat. I think you'll like it" said Anderek, and he led the way through a narrow door.

The restaurant was small, with immaculately clean and starched white tablecloths, minimal decor and spartan wooden chairs. A waiter showed them to a table against the wall at the back of the room.

"In Slovakia we usually eat our main meal at lunchtime, but European habits are slowly creeping into our culture and dinner's becoming a fashion item". The tone of Anderek's voice had just a hint of disapproval.

Salter ran his gaze down the large triptych menu the waiter had handed to him. "As long as I get to try something typically Slovakian. The guide book had a lot to say about your national cuisine and just hearing about it made me ravenous".

Anderek smiled encouragingly at him.

"You won't be disappointed with the food here, I can assure you. Let me recommend the pork dish. Third one down, centre page".

Salter followed the directions, noting the brief description printed in English. "Yes, I think I'll go for that. It looks good".

"That's settled then" said Anderek, folding his menu and putting it flat on the small table. "And if you have no objection, I'll choose the wine as well. They have a Hungarian red here that you can't seem to get anywhere else. Much to be recommended, and I speak from experience".

Salter nodded agreement.

A few minutes later, Anderek had ordered and they were sitting over their aperitif, an excellent and very cold dry white wine.

"So tell me a bit more about this magical mystery tour I seem to be on. You've been very cagey so far".

Anderek laughed loudly and slapped his hand on the edge of the table. Then he picked up his wine glass and took a large mouthful.

"You're absolutely right! I've been very 'cagey', as you say, and I meant to be. I didn't want to spoil your first trip out here by giving things away. Tomorrow's going to be a wonderful surprise for you. Yanik will be driving us again and he knows the best routes to anywhere in this country".

He took another mouthful of wine, smaller this time.
"We are heading for the Presov region. It's a particularly beautiful area in the north east. I don't know how much your guide book told you but Presov is one of the twelve regions of Slovakia. It's very popular with the bureaucrats at the moment and they've got their eye on it for economic development and that kind of thing. There's a growing tourist industry, although it hasn't spoiled the natural beauty of the place. It's still one of

the 'less settled' parts of the country, as they say, and if some of us have our way, it'll stay like that".

The waiter appeared with hors d'oeuvres and the Hungarian wine. Anderek briefly muttered his thanks and continued talking.

"The region has the High Tatras Mountains. One of the peaks is the highest point in Slovakia. Two thousand six hundred and fifty-five metres to be precise. You won't be surprised to hear there's a lot of skiing in the winter. It's really amazing to look at".

"But what's the particular spot we're making for?" said Salter, finishing the white wine and sipping the red the waiter had poured.

"The town of Presov itself. It's the third largest town in the whole country. It's just over four hundred kilometres from here, so we won't have too much time for sightseeing, not if we're going to get back in a day. But I hope to show you some of the more interesting sights from the comfort of our car."

Salter drank some more of the red wine, noting how good it was.

"Can you tell me a bit more about this document? When we met, I believe you said it was still being dated".

His tone was deliberately decisive. The shortage of information was beginning to irritate him and he felt it was time to take charge of this whole thing. He looked directly into the other man's eyes as he spoke.

Anderek stared back at him. Then he nodded gravely.

"Things have moved on since our first meeting, Father Salter. Our experts have carried out further tests".

"Who are these experts?"

Anderek took the interruption in his stride. "We have our own at the Institute and we've had some help from the National Museum and one of our linked universities. There have been comparisons with other ancient documents and two fragments have been carbon dated independently".

"So what's the result?"

"It is as we originally thought. The document is fourth century. We can now be certain of that". Anderek leaned back in his chair and folded his arms, as if to underline the finality of what he had just said.

"Right" said Salter, aware that he was only playing for time as he thought what to say next.

"And how would you describe it? Is it a book of some kind?"

Anderek drank some of the red wine, then topped Salter's glass up and then his own.

"Unfortunately, there are only a few pages left of what seems to have been a sizeable piece of literature. Today I believe it would be called a hagiography".

"A life of the saints" said Salter, impressed once again not only with Anderek's command of English but also his technical knowledge.

"Yes, I think so. The names of some other New Testament figures also appear in the fragments that have survived, notably that of St Peter. Its theme may have been the expansion of the Early Church".

"When you say 'fragments', how much of it's left?"

"Nine pages, most of them in reasonably good condition for their age. And it's a miracle of providence we have these, when you consider how they got to us".

These last words seemed to hang in the air and Salter waited to see what would follow them. "What do you mean by that?" he said finally.

The waiter appeared again, this time with the main course. For a few moments they ate in silence. Then Anderek put his knife and fork down and rested his elbows on the table, holding the tips of his fingers loosely together.

"It's time to introduce you to someone else. Someone who has played a key part in this drama. Fr Vasiloff Zaborska is a priest of the Byzantine Catholic Church. You are familiar with that particular branch of Christendom?"

"Not directly". For a few seconds, Salter floundered. He was once again in a situation where he needed to match Anderek's knowledge. Church history was something he had always found boring beyond words.

"Presumably they're one of the Uniate churches. In communion with Rome and acknowledging the authority of the Pope but keeping their Orthodox traditions and their liturgy".

"Precisely" said Anderek, and his tone was that of a headmaster giving measured praise to a bright pupil.

"Fr Zaborska is an old man now. He has worked all his life in Slovakia. And he knows what it means to be persecuted. The communists were suspicious of Byzantine Orthodox Christians, and particularly their priests. They always regarded them as potential spies because of their allegiance to the Vatican. He was arrested and tortured on a number of occasions".

"And was he a spy?"

Anderek picked up the knife and fork and cut into his meal again. "Well I don't know for sure. If he was, he hasn't told me.

He is certainly a great patriot. He loves Slovakia. But I think he was just a priest who did what he thought was right. In any case, the communists never needed an excuse for imprisoning anyone".

Salter finished chewing a large mouthful of the pork. He almost regretted having to talk over such a delicious meal.

"So did he find the document?"

"He didn't find it because for him it was always there. When he was young, he learned of its existence from older priests who had spent their entire lives protecting it and moving it from one place to another, so that it shouldn't fall into the wrong hands. By then, most of it had already been lost or destroyed. Then one day, the task fell to him. All those who knew about it, who had kept it hidden in their monasteries and churches, had died. He sealed it in a wooden box and hid it away in his own church, and there it stayed for many years. Decades, in fact. Sadly, during that time, one of the surviving pages disintegrated, leaving the nine we have now."

Anderek paused to finish the wine in his glass.

"Fr Zaborska eventually became worried about the document and its condition. He's no scientist, he's a simple man. But he's no fool either and he knew he couldn't do what was needed to preserve it from further deterioration. And he'd heard about the traffic in stolen art treasures and he was naturally concerned for its safety. So he came to us".

"How did he find you?"

"He confided in a friend who was a teacher and who just happened to know about the Institute".

"So does Fr Zaborska understand the importance of this document? I mean the connection between St Paul and

England and these stone triangles. Does he know about all that?"

"He does now, because it's all been carefully explained to him. And he has some grasp of Latin".

Salter was about to put his wine glass to his lips. Then he stopped, holding the glass in mid air.

"Did you say 'Latin'? I'd assumed it was written in Slavonic".

Anderek smiled and raised his eyebrows slightly.

"Slavonic as a written language developed quite late, around the early Middle Ages. What we now call Slovakia was a province of the Roman Empire. So whatever dialects the natives spoke then, the official language would have been Latin. And we know that there were Christians in the Roman army and civil service. The document could be the work of an educated Roman Christian".

Salter nodded slowly and drank a mouthful of wine.

"In any case" Anderek continued "who ever said the document originated in ancient Slovakia? It could just as easily have been written in Rome or any city of the Empire and brought here later by missionaries".

Not for the first time that evening, Salter felt he was behind the game and he mentally cursed himself for not thinking the matter through and working a few details out in advance. Anderek looked at him and gave him the usual reassuring smile.

They finished eating and the waiter appeared again with the dessert menu, which they both declined. Anderek ordered coffee.

"And now, Father Salter, let's look ahead. If you are satisfied with what you see tomorrow and you wish to proceed with things, and I am not making any assumptions even at this advanced stage, then we must consider what your role will be in this whole project as it develops". Anderek was leaning on the table again, the tips of his fingers placed loosely together in an attitude of complete relaxation and confidence. Salter was listening intently.

"If it all works out and our investigations in Hadleigh Bridge reveal what we believe is there, then we will need a consultant with background knowledge of the Church of England and how it works administratively. The sort of person who could help us not to, how would you put it, tread on toes. I believe you, Father Salter, would be the obvious person. You could negotiate some arrangement with the Institute whereby you worked for us part-time, or even full-time. We could discuss your salary and I'm sure there would be European funding available. The EU can be very generous when it comes to projects like this one".

The coffee arrived. Salter scarcely noticed it as he waited for Anderek to continue.

"The Ministry of Education has properties in Bratislava, including a number of flats near the city centre reserved for important overseas visitors. One of these could be made available to you whenever you wanted it. And of course the Institute would pay for your travel to and from England. How do you feel about that, my dear Father?"

Salter took a deep breath, then slowly let it out. What he had just heard seemed unreal. A new life with the kind of opportunities he had only dreamed of so far was being presented to him on a plate. It was all incredibly easy. Or was it too easy?

"Don't answer yet!" said Anderek. His tone was jovial. "It's a lot to take in, I know. I can hardly believe it myself. But tomorrow you will see the document and you will meet Fr Zaborska. He has very little English, but he is a wonderful personality and you will like him at once, I am sure".

He gestured to the waiter to bring the bill.

At the main entrance door to the Carmen Hotel, Anderek shook Salter's hand warmly and wished him goodnight. Then he waited for him to go in.

Salter took the lift up to his room. He took his jacket off, threw it on the bed and walked over to the window. Drawing the curtains back, he looked down on the pedestrian area where the street lights glowed softly.

He took his shirt off and unlaced his shoes. Then he stood for a moment and looked at himself in the room's full-length mirror. Was he still young? he wondered. Yes, he decided, he probably was. Although he wouldn't be for much longer. He still had time. But the day would come when he would suddenly realise he hadn't got any more time. And there was always the danger it would come before he was ready for it.

He opened the mini bar found a single malt scotch and poured it into a glass tumbler. Then he swallowed it down in one gulp. He couldn't afford to miss an opportunity like this, he thought. It wouldn't come again. And if he let it go by, then he'd spend the rest of his life regretting it. And that could ruin whatever else he did. Sure there might be risks involved. But anything that was worth anything had a risk of some kind attached to it.

Anderek wasn't pushing him into anything, and he felt reassured by that. He wasn't in a trap of any kind. He could say no anytime he wanted to. But he wouldn't. He was sure of that now. This was his big chance in life and he was going to take it with both hands.

Now what would he need for tomorrow? They'd agreed to meet at eight so he would have breakfast soon after seven. He'd wear the jeans he'd travelled in and his leather coat, and maybe the lightweight sweater. Pity he had no camera. Anderek had said he'd prefer him not to take photographs so he'd left it behind.

He brushed his teeth and spent several minutes flicking through the channels on the television. Then he switched the light out and got into bed, and was soon asleep.

. . .

The man who called himself Stefanov Anderek watched him as he walked through reception and into the lift. He needed to know where this man was at any time, so he made sure he was heading for his room. Then he lit a cigarette, turned and strolled along the pedestrian area. At the edge of a busy street he stopped and took out his mobile and called someone somewhere. What he said would have been completely meaningless to anyone who heard it. He talked about the meal he had just had and how much his old friend had enjoyed it. He said he hoped that he and the recipient of the call could meet up again some time, and to these sentiments he added a few trivial details, finishing with a cheerful goodbye.

It was a coded message saying that everything was ready for the next stage of the operation and that this would take place tomorrow, exactly as it had been planned.

The silver grey BMW pulled up in front of him with Yanik at the wheel. He got in and the car sped away.

Chapter 14

Gavin Salter relaxed in the now familiar comfort of the BMW's back seat. He was only vaguely aware of Anderek's voice describing the fertile lowlands of southern Slovakia and the mountainous regions of the north.

Breakfast in the hotel had been the lavish affair he had expected, with an enormous buffet offering every possible combination of gourmet food. He had lingered over the rich dark coffee, watching as wealthy tourists overloaded their plates and wondering how much food was wasted there on an average day. Still, this was not the time or place to worry about principles, he thought as he looked out of the car's rear window. He was here to have a good time. And he was going to do just that.

Yanik was a fast driver. They were on a main road and the traffic was moving, but he still felt the need to overtake any vehicle that dared to be in front of him. "Manic Yanik" he decided to call him. The green landscape glided by and occasionally he caught sight of a village with red-roofed houses. He had left the guide book in the hotel room, but he remembered what it had said about Slovakia retaining its history and folk traditions, and being a bit less glitzy than some of its famous neighbours. Now how about some of these castles and fortresses? he thought, looking across the fields at the distant hills. What did the book say? " ... recalling turbulent moments from the country's past and the frequent ... "

"Mind if I smoke?" Anderek interrupted his thoughts.

"Go ahead".

Anderek lit a Marlboro with the electronic lighter. "Bad habit, I know. But it always helps me relax". He drew heavily, inhaling the smoke deep into his lungs, then slowly breathing it out. Salter guessed he must smoke quite a lot and wondered why he'd not seen him smoke until now. Just being considerate, he concluded.

"So who are we due to meet when we get there?"

Anderek flicked ash into one of the car's ashtrays. "Two of my colleagues from the Institute. Gerdovich Hanacek is an archaeologist and graphologist. He's not well known outside Slovakia, but here he is a recognised authority in his field. And Dr Maslar Janovic is an expert in the New Testament and the history of the Early Church. He's written a number of books and he's a visiting lecturer at several of our universities. And of course Fr Zaborska. Although you shouldn't expect him to contribute too much to our discussions".

"And we're meeting where? At Fr Zaborska's church?"

"No!" Anderek laughed. "His church is even further away! And the journey would take us over some very rough terrain!" He drew on the cigarette again.

"We've booked a meeting space in the town's library. It's a small and very modest room, but enough for our needs".

Salter felt his curiosity growing. Something didn't quite fit, he thought.

"If Fr Zaborska's church is a long way away and the Institute's in Bratislava, where's the connection with Presov?"

"It's merely a question of convenience. We needed somewhere we could all get to without too much trouble" said Anderek. "And I have one or two contacts in the town. In any case, we felt we couldn't ask Fr Zaborska to travel too far. Like I said, he's an old man". Another draw on the cigarette. Even heavier this time.

"And what about the document? How is it being transported from the Institute?"

Anderek shifted slightly in the seat. "The document has never been held at the Institute. We have secure storage in Presov, which I arranged myself with the local authorities".

"But didn't you say your experts had been running tests on it?"

Anderek took a deep breath and held it for a moment. Salter noted that he had never seen him do that before. A crack seemed to have appeared in his usual composure.

"The comparison with other ancient texts did not require the presence of the document itself. Close-up photographs were sufficient. The carbon dating tests were done with very small fragments taken from the disintegrated page".

Salter nodded reflectively.

"Didn't I read something about a university at Presov? Why aren't they involved in this project? Could you not have used their expertise or their facilities in some way?"

Anderek leaned forward and stubbed the cigarette out in the ashtray. He spoke without lifting his gaze.

"They are not one of our linked universities". Then he turned his head and stared out of the rear window.

Salter could see Anderek was uncomfortable with his questions. Maybe he had just asked one question too many. But his curiosity remained.

. . .

The BMW pulled into a side street and parked. Gavin Salter blinked and rubbed his eyes. The air conditioning had made the atmosphere in the car hot and dry and for the last hour or so he had been close to falling asleep. He got out and stood on the pavement, stretching his limbs. It was colder than it had been in Bratislava, he noticed, and the air was clean and bracing. He took a few deep breaths to wake himself up.

"Welcome to Presov" said Anderek, lighting another cigarette. "The library's not far from here". He led the way, while Yanik walked several paces behind them. He knows his place, thought Salter.

They turned into a wide street and Salter got his first impression of the city of Presov. The high terraced buildings were tastefully ornate and painted in pastel colours and the street was edged by grass verges and carefully cultivated flowerbeds. The civic pride was unmistakeable and he thought of the Prague Spring of 1968 and the early ripples of opposition to communism in the former Czechoslovakia. And he remembered reading that support for the reforms came mainly from people in the towns, while country dwellers favoured the status quo. What about these people? he wondered. Where did their sympathies lie? Were they ready to go to the barricades?

They walked in silence and he noticed that Anderek was in sombre mood and not at all his usual self. Maybe he was suffering the effects of the journey as well, he thought.

Predictably, the library was one of the high, pastel-coloured buildings. Its yellow and white façade had a kind of chocolate-box appeal, thought Salter. Anderek went ahead through the wooden entrance door and it creaked and rattled as he opened it. As the three of them walked in, Anderek muttered a few words over his shoulder to Yanik, and Yanik grunted something barely audible in reply.

The library's entrance hall was neat, clean and spartan. A smell of floor polish and disinfectant hung in the air. Anderek walked quickly up to the reception desk and said something to the young woman standing behind it. She nodded and then led the way down a corridor, stopping in front of a glass panelled door. Then she turned and walked back along the corridor. Anderek opened the door and stood aside to let Salter enter the room.

The first thing he saw was a long trestle table standing in the centre of the room. On it stood three large flat cardboard boxes.

"So, this must be the famous Father Gavin Salter".

He turned in the direction of the voice, and something immediately unsettled him. It was the way the three men were standing. They were forming a kind of tableau. And it was close to being menacing.

"Indeed you are right, Dr Janovic" said Anderek, identifying the owner of the voice.

Janovic stepped forward, his right hand extended. He was a well-built man, perhaps in his fifties, with a full head of thick, iron grey hair and bushy eyebrows. His jaw was square and deep lines showed around his eyes and on his forehead.

He might well have been handsome when he was younger. The shabby grey suit and unpolished shoes were the uniform of an academic and his bodily movements were awkward, suggesting embarrassment and even a lack of confidence.

"It is very good to meet you at last" he said in slow, hesitant English. "We have heard much about your interest in our project and we are grateful for it".

Salter was about to reply when Anderek interrupted.

"And this is Gerdovich Hanacek. As I explained, he is the project's archaeologist and graphologist".

Hanacek was a thin and wiry man aged around forty with a pointed chin and small dark eyes. His head was completely bald. He looked quietly stylish in a well-cut black suit and black polo shirt buttoned to the neck. His expression was emotionless and gave nothing away, although he managed the merest trace of a smile as he shook hands and muttered Salter's name.

"And of course, this is Fr Zaborska" said Anderek.

Draped in an all-enveloping black cassock, Fr Zaborska was the perfect stereotype of an eastern-church priest, Salter thought. His rugged and weather-beaten face was that of a peasant. The wild, unruly beard was grey, flecked here and there with black, and his mouth was almost completely hidden by it. If he was as old as Anderek had implied, he certainly didn't look it, and his thick black hair was pushed back over his head and grew closely round his ears. The dark blue eyes stared intently.

Salter had never met an Orthodox priest before, having seen them only on one or two formal occasions and always at a polite distance. And he certainly hadn't come into contact with a Byzantine Catholic. He wondered nervously whether there was a protocol of some kind that he ought to know about and the thought briefly crossed his mind that they might have a special handshake, like the Freemasons. Then he dismissed the thought as silly.

He grasped the large, rough hand that was being offered to him and Fr Zaborska smiled, his uneven teeth only just showing through the gap in his beard. Then he spoke, and the deep guttural sound was totally incomprehensible.

Salter stared blankly back at him, wondering what to do next. Then suddenly he realised the man had said, "Christ is Risen!" and he mentally cursed himself for not recognising the traditional greeting.

"He is risen indeed!" said Salter, making the customary reply.

Fr Zaborska threw his head back in a burst of laughter and clasped Salter's hand in both of his.

"Well, I'm pleased you reverend gentlemen have finally met" said Anderek, stepping into the centre of the group. "Now let us get straight down to work. We are all busy men". He gestured towards the trestle table.

Yanik had meanwhile transferred the three cardboard boxes to a smaller table in one corner of the room and the trestle table now had a length of green baize spread over its surface. He took the lids off the cardboard boxes and stacked them neatly on the floor. Then, as if by some prearranged signal, Janovic and Hanacek crossed the room and began removing the contents of the boxes, slowly and carefully, with a solemnity that was almost religious, and placing the objects on the green baize. When they had finished, they stood back. The room was in complete silence.

Nine wooden frames, each one about an inch and a half deep, were arranged in a straight line on the table. The glass in the frames was clear and highly polished and reflected the light from the room's high windows. At first, no-one moved.

"Please, Father Salter" said Anderek, gesturing again towards the table. "Take a closer look. This is what you have been patiently waiting to see".

Salter walked over to the table and went slowly along the line. He was acutely aware of eyes watching him, gauging his reaction.

The pages in the frames were of a dull beige colour, darker at the edges where they appeared to have deteriorated. Each page was covered with a small script. The writing looked faded and in places it was all but invisible. He bent over one of the frames and peered closely at the text. Once or twice he thought he could identify one of the tiny letters but he was completely unable to make out any words.

Janovic and Hanacek now stepped forward and stood either side of him.

"The material is parchment" said Hanacek. "We have reason to believe it is of a particularly good quality". Except for the barely audible greeting when they had met, Hanacek had not spoken before. His English pronunciation was good, but the voice was a flat monotone.

"The script is, of course, difficult to read with the naked eye" said Janovic. "To decipher it we have used various technologies, including computer enhancement".

Salter nodded, slowly and thoughtfully. For a moment there was silence in the room again. Then Hanacek spoke.

"And even when the text itself is made clearly visible, most of it is difficult to understand. A fourth century writer would not necessarily have written words exactly as we do. And in the ancient world, writing generally was far less stylised than it is today. Much more, what is the English word, idiosyncratic?"

"Yes, I understand" said Salter. Again silence.

"Here and there it is possible to make out words" said Janovic. "Can you see the name Paulus ?" He pointed with his finger to a word on one of the pages. Salter followed Janovic's finger. The word was just about visible.

"And here is the word Britannia". He pointed to another of the pages. "This is in fact the section that includes the geographical references to Southern England".

Salter bent over the frame and examined the text. Again following Janovic's finger, he saw a word beginning with a capital "B". It might conceivably have been Britannia, he thought. But the other words on the page were completely indecipherable.

"Is there a translation I could see?"

"Of course, Father Salter" said Anderek from behind him. "We are working on a full English translation at this very moment and very shortly now we will be able to let you have a copy. Hopefully before you travel back to England. I am expecting to hear from my colleagues at the Institute any time now".

Salter took a deep breath, then let it out slowly. He was beginning to feel confused and slightly frustrated.

"To be honest, I find this all very strange. You seem to be asking me to make some kind of judgement on an ancient manuscript which I've never seen before and which I know nothing about, except what you've told me".

Anderek crossed the room and stood beside him. Once again, there was a genuine warmth in the hand that he placed on Salter's shoulder.

"I understand, Father Salter" he said in a soft, almost tender voice. "You must feel we're putting you in a very difficult position. But just ask yourself this. Could this whole thing be a hoax? Have we really brought you all this way just to make a fool of you?"

Salter nodded. There was an irresistible logic in what Anderek said, and he felt himself being carried along by it. Something inside him wanted it all to be true.

"Yes, you're right. There wouldn't be any purpose in that at all, would there?" And as he said the words, he felt himself giving way.

Suddenly there was a sense of relaxation in the room. Anderek and the other three men were all smiling at him, encouragingly.

"So gentlemen" said Anderek, taking command. "I believe our first meeting has been a success. You, Father Salter, have seen what you came here to see. And we have had the chance to lay the evidence before you and to make our case to you. I'm sure you feel the strength of our convictions. Now you know how firmly we believe in this project. I suggest we now spend some time getting to know each other socially".

Again as if a signal had been prearranged, Janovic and Hanacek moved swiftly to the trestle table, while Yanik gathered up the cardboard boxes. The frames were replaced in their packaging with careful precision and the green baize folded. The table now looked just as it had when they came in, with the three boxes standing on it.

"I hope you will excuse Fr Zaborska" said Anderek. "He is a busy man, as a fellow priest like yourself will appreciate. And now he must return to his parish".

With another firm handshake and a wordless inclination of the head, Fr Zaborska left the room. His footsteps were heard as he walked quickly down the corridor. Then the sound of them faded and he was gone.

"I think we should get some food" said Janovic. "I'm very hungry and it's past lunchtime. What do you English say, Father Salter? I could eat a horse!"

He laughed self-consciously. The other three men politely joined in his laughter.

Chapter 15

The restaurant off the main square of the town was an expensive one. Lunch was nearly over and only a few of the tables in the lavishly furnished dining room were occupied. At Anderek's insistence, they had eaten their way through a heavy meal of soup and meat dishes and were now finishing dessert. Several bottles of Golden Pheasant beer had been consumed and Gavin Salter was beginning to feel sleepy.

Throughout the meal, Anderek had questioned him about St Mary's, about Hadleigh Bridge, about the Sunday services and the people who came to them, about the Church of England and about religion in Britain. Anderek had dominated the conversation, while Janovic and Hanacek had scarcely spoken a word.

The dessert dishes were now empty. Anderek took his cigarettes and lighter out of his jacket pocket, put them on the table and looked at his watch. He called the waiter and ordered coffee.

"So where to from here?" said Salter. He was now finding it hard to focus and with some effort he managed to suppress a yawn.

Anderek lit a cigarette and inhaled the smoke deeply.

"I think you should give yourself time before making your final decision".

"Do I need any more time?" said Salter. "I've already told you I've no reason to doubt what I've seen today".

Anderek drew deeply on the cigarette again.

"It's very reassuring to hear you say that, Father Salter and I'm glad that you feel that way. But even so, I would like you to give yourself more time to reflect on what we have shown you, and on the things you and I have discussed. I want the decision to be yours and yours alone, and I want you to be able to justify it to yourself".

"We would be happier if you took your time" said Hanacek, unexpectedly breaking into the conversation and speaking in his usual monotone. "We are confident that you will want to work with us, but we do not want you to feel you have made a decision under pressure of any kind".

The waiter arrived with coffee in large white cups. Salter picked up the spoon from the saucer and stirred the dark, steaming liquid. Pale froth swirled on the surface and the aroma was delicious. He hoped the caffeine would wake him up.

"Well, I suppose you're right. After all, it's what you might call a leap of faith". He lifted the cup to his mouth.

Janovic laughed and leaned back in his chair.

"Well, you know what St Paul said. 'Faith is the substance of things hoped for, the certainty of what we cannot see'".

Salter froze. The cup was just touching his lower lip.

"I'm sorry, Dr Janovic?" he said, still holding the cup in mid air.

"Faith is the substance of things hoped for" repeated Janovic. "Hebrews! Paul's Epistle to the Hebrews!"

"Oh ... er ... yes, of course. Hebrews" said Salter. "Chapter eleven, verse one, isn't it?" He looked across at Janovic and smiled.

Janovic laughed again. "Absolutely right, Father Salter!"

Salter took a large mouthful of coffee. It was very hot and it slightly burnt his tongue. Out of the corner of his eye, he could see that Anderek was staring at him.

They finished the meal in silence, except for a few words from Anderek about Yanik bringing the car to the front of the restaurant.

Salter barely registered what Anderek had said. He was wide awake now.

And his mind was racing.

...

The BMW drew up by the hotel. It was dark and the street lamps in front of the Carmen glowed mistily. Anderek and Salter got out. Yanik stayed sitting at the wheel without turning his head.

"It's been a long day" said Anderek. "You must now have a good night's sleep".

"Thanks, it's all been very interesting" said Salter, and they shook hands.

"Tomorrow I want you to meet some more colleagues from the Institute and they can tell you more about our work. I'll pick you up at about ten".

Anderek got into the front passenger seat and the car pulled away.

"Something's not right" he said to Yanik. "I must make sure

he is watched carefully".

He took out his mobile.

. . .

Gavin Salter slammed the door of the hotel room behind him so hard that objects in the room shook. He suddenly felt the need to release the energy which had now been pent up inside him for several hours and taking his leather coat off he threw it with force. It crashed into one of the chairs and slid into a crumpled heap on the floor.

He opened the mini bar and put ice into a glass. Then he unzipped his suitcase and took out the bottle of scotch he had brought with him meaning to keep it in reserve. He poured a large measure over the ice and tipped half of it down his throat.

He sat on the edge of the bed, his elbows resting on his knees, the glass held in both hands.

An expert in the New Testament and Early Church history, who calls himself "doctor", writes books and lectures at universities. And thinks St Paul is the author of the Letter to the Hebrews.

He ran the thought through his mind several times. It was as if he needed to convince himself of what he'd heard.

He took a sip of the whiskey. Perhaps he was overreacting. Shouldn't Janovic be allowed his opinion, even if it was an eccentric one? But then how could any scholar in any respectable university think that Paul wrote Hebrews? That notion had been abandoned decades ago. Not even the fundamentalists thought it was tenable.

Had it been a genuine mistake? Even the experts get things wrong sometimes, especially when they've been knocking back the alcohol. But no real New Testament scholar could make a mistake like that. And in any case, he'd picked him up on it. Janovic had been given the chance to put himself right. But he hadn't taken it.

There was no other conclusion. Janovic was a fake. He must have memorised a few well-known quotes from the Bible just to give himself credibility. And that one he hadn't researched properly.

He took another sip of the whiskey, stood up and walked over to the window, looking down on the trees and the streetlamps. Then the questions started coming with terrifying speed.

If Janovic was a fake, then what about the others? Who were they? What the hell was going on here? What had he got himself into?

Why had Janovic and Hanacek said so little during the meal? Anderek had kept him busy with a whole string of questions about his parish and the work he did. In fact, he'd found it difficult to keep up with Anderek's questioning. Was that so he wouldn't have a chance to ask the other two about what they did? Was Anderek afraid they'd give themselves away?

Who was this "Father Zaborska"? He clearly wasn't as old as Anderek had made him out to be. And what proof was there that he was really a priest? Conveniently he didn't speak English! Was that to guard against awkward questions? And was he a Byzantine Catholic for the same reason? Because it was an obscure church and a lot less was known about it in the West, so that it would be harder to spot the deception? In any case, he hadn't had the chance to speak to him. He'd just disappeared.

What was the real reason for their trip almost to the other end of Slovakia? He'd noticed that Anderek had become jumpy in the car, suddenly smoking like an addict and not liking it very much when he was asked questions. Was the idea to get as far away from Bratislava as possible? Were they just covering up the fact that there was no Institute for Historical and Cultural Research, in Bratislava or anywhere else?

And this supposedly ancient document? All he had seen was a few lines of illegible script. Only two words in the whole thing were anything like visible. And they just happened to be the two words that verified what they were telling him. And they'd been quick to point that out.

But then what about the Institute's website? He'd seen it for himself. It was all there that day he'd logged onto it. And he'd checked it against the websites of other Slovakian government ministries and it looked alright. The addresses and phone numbers had all lined up. And what about the email to Anderek's secretary? She'd replied to it within half an hour.

For a moment he wondered if he was being completely paranoid. Maybe there was a logical explanation for everything that had happened.

But then, he thought, anyone with the technical know-how could set up a bogus website. And how could he tell where the email had gone or who had replied to it?

Suddenly he felt he was in a nightmare world of fantasy and pretence. Nothing in it had any substance and there was no proof that anything was what it claimed to be. Anderek's subtle powers of suggestion had brainwashed him into thinking it couldn't possibly be an elaborate scam. But now he could see that was exactly what it was. And what was the purpose of it?

And then, the most terrifying question of all forced itself to the front of his mind. If he went along with this any further and got any more involved than he already was, what would happen to him?

He finished the scotch and threw the half-melted ice down the sink. Then he put fresh ice in the glass and poured another one, smaller this time. He sat on the bed again.

He knew he had to think clearly now and plan every step carefully. They, whoever "they" were, could be watching him at any time. And if they thought for a moment that he suspected anything, God knows what they might do.

His only option, he decided, was to get away as quickly as possible. He could forget the airport. If the worst happened and they decided to go after him, that would be the first place they would look. And he could be delayed there for hours waiting for a flight. It would have to be a train to the nearest large city and from there he could sort out his journey back to England and safety.

He felt like taking a shower but decided that would take too long. He unbuttoned his shirt and took it off. In the bathroom he splashed cold water on his face, neck and chest, then brushed his teeth. He quickly packed his clothes and the bottle of scotch into the suitcase. Then he put his shirt back on, briefly checked the room to see he had packed everything and picked up the key. He walked along the corridor to the lift.

In the lift, he looked at himself in the mirror. He was alright, he thought. He didn't look so stressed he would attract attention. The lift reached the ground floor and he stepped out into the reception area.

The hotel was quiet and only a few people wandered across

the black-and-white tiled floor on the way back to their rooms after an evening's enjoyment. Don't panic, he thought. Just stay calm. All you're doing is checking out of a hotel. People do it all the time. No-one's even going to notice.

He collapsed the handle of the suitcase and stood it behind one of the armchairs. Then he wandered slowly over to the reception desk and started looking nonchalantly through the leaflets in the wall rack. He found a train timetable, unfolded it and spread it out on the polished surface of the desk. Running his finger down the columns of figures, he noted there was a train to Vienna at twenty-one twenty. He checked his watch. Just under an hour. Could he get there in time? How far was the station? How long would he have to wait for a taxi? Stay calm, he thought.

He walked across to the seating area, retrieved his suitcase and walked back to the reception desk. The boyish looking young man with closely cropped hair who had been busy tapping the keyboard of the PC now stared at him, his face blank and unsmiling, and raised an eyebrow.

"I'd like to check out, please" said Salter speaking in a low voice.

The young man nodded.

"Your room number?"

Salter passed him the key and he tapped the keyboard again.

"Father Salter" he said and looked at him out of the corner of his eye with just a hint of curiosity. "Your bill and all your expenses have been paid in advance".

"Yes, of course" said Salter, mentally kicking himself. He should have guessed they would have had that sorted already.

"We weren't expecting you to leave till the weekend" said the young man, raising one eyebrow again. "Would you like me to contact Mr Anderek?"

His heart leapt.

"No!" he snapped, then took a breath. "No, thank you. That won't be necessary. Not at this late hour. I'll be in contact with him myself tomorrow".

"I hope your stay with us has been satisfactory" said the young man, this time with just the trace of a smile.

"Yes" said Salter, feeling strained and trying hard to put some warmth into his voice. "I have been very comfortable here and I would certainly recommend you. It's just that I had a call earlier and I need to leave immediately".

That seemed to satisfy the young man. Again he made the trace of a smile.

"Which station?" he said and picked up the desk phone.

. . .

The metallic blue taxi sped south over the New Bridge towards Bratislava Petrzalka station. At any other time, Salter would have been nervous about driving at such a speed, but now he was grateful.

While he had waited, he had sat in one of the armchairs and read a magazine someone had left behind, trying hard to look and feel relaxed. He had told himself that no-one was watching him and that the very idea was absurd. But he was not convinced, and having positioned himself so that he could see the door, threw the occasional furtive glance towards the cobble-stoned street outside. The taxi had taken just ten minutes to arrive and the burly unshaven taxi driver had thrown his suitcase into the boot with an incomprehensible grunt. Salter had said the name of the station, but the man hadn't acknowledged the instruction in any way.

The journey took only a few minutes. The taxi screeched to a halt at the station's main entrance and the driver got out and removed the suitcase from the boot. Salter glanced at the taxi's meter and, with a quick calculation, presented the man with a handful of notes sufficient to cover the charge and a generous tip. With the same grunt he had given at the hotel and without looking up, he took the money, climbed back into the taxi and sped away.

With his credit card and the help of a kindly, English-speaking Slovakian woman, he bought a single ticket to the Vienna Südbahnhof, then followed the illuminated signs to the platform. The train, with its red and white coaches, had already arrived and passengers were streaming out of its doors. Salter stood still for a brief moment and sighed with genuine relief.

. . .

The room was lit by a single bare light bulb. It was quiet and from the warehouse on the other side of the door, the sound of water dripping from leaking pipes could clearly be heard.

"So what kind of a useless fucking arsehole are you?"
Anderek brought his fist down with a crash on the surface of the table. The man sitting on the steel tubular chair jumped at the noise, then shifted uncomfortably.

Yanik stood by the door, motionless, his hands held behind his back.

"Look ... I ... I have already said I'm sorry. It was a mistake. I know that" the man stammered, beads of sweat appearing on his forehead. "I must have fallen asleep when I sat down on the bench. It was only for a minute or two. It was late. I must have been hanging around that hotel for hours".

"A minute or two?" repeated Anderek and brought his fist down on the table again, harder this time. "That was enough time for the bastard to slip away! If we'd known he was planning to run, we could have picked him up then and disposed of him! Instead we're in this fucking mess!"

Anderek's voice rose almost to a scream. The man was visibly frightened.

"Alright, I admit I screwed up" he said, his throat now so tight he could barely get the words out. "But if I hadn't thought to check with hotel reception, we might not have found out till morning!" He wiped a handful of sweat from his forehead with one hand.

"Congratulations on using your brain for once" said Anderek, the words dripping with venomous sarcasm.

The man bent over the table and buried his face in his hands. Anderek lit a cigarette and began to pace up and down, his heels clicking on the stone floor of the room.

"Get back to the hotel. Find out when the taxi left and where it was going. I want to know in half an hour".

Anderek leaned across the table and held the burning tip of the cigarette close to the man's face. The man looked at the cigarette. Then his eyes met Anderek's gaze.

"You're lucky to have got away with this" said Anderek, slowly and softly, carefully measuring each word. "You won't get away with it again. I think you know what the organisation does to pieces of shit like you".

The man swallowed audibly. More sweat appeared on his forehead.

Anderek stood up straight and gestured towards the door with one finger. The man leapt out of the chair as if he had been electrocuted and threw himself at the door. Yanik only just managed to open the door before the man crashed into it.

Chapter 16

The train drew into Vienna's Südbahnhof. There had been a delay in Bratislava caused by some kind of technical trouble and Salter had spent an anxious fifteen minutes wondering if he'd been followed and whether the delay would mean they'd find him. He had peered out of the windows several times, while at the same time trying not to make himself too visible. Finally he had heard the shrill sound of a whistle and a guard's voice shouting, and the train had pulled away.

He yawned and stretched his arms. He was suddenly tired and after the stress of the last few hours, his muscles and joints had begun to ache. He looked at his watch. It was nearly ten forty-five and he hoped he could find somewhere to stay quickly. He was in no mood for walking around Vienna for hours, however romantic the place might be.

In the booking hall he spotted a uniform and to his great relief, the man spoke reasonably good English. The word "hotel" was enough to elicit clear and comprehensive directions and stepping out onto the main street, he found the left hand turn the man had indicated and headed south for Laxenburger Strasse.

The Hotel Marlbeck was clearly not in the same league as

the one he had recently left and he guessed it catered for small-time business travellers. The reception area was neat and clean and dominated by an enormous rubber plant, and a cheap gold-framed mirror hung on the wall next to it. An overweight middle-aged woman, her grey hair tied back and fixed in a tight bun, glared at him from behind the reception desk. She stood up as he approached and spoke to her.

"Good evening" he said to her, smiling broadly and hoping he wouldn't have to make use of whatever German he could still remember from his school days. "I'm sorry to arrive so late, but I would very much like a room for the night if you have one".

She continued to glare at him and he was about to say something even more apologetic when she spoke.

"The rooms are available Monday to Friday, from seven thirty to twenty hundred hours".

Her English was slow and laboured. She could have been reading from a brochure and he found himself glancing at the surface of the desk to see if she was.

"Yes, of course" he said, looking wearily down at the floor and working hard to keep up the apologetic tone. "I realise it's very late and you have your rules, but is it possible that ... "

Another slow and laboured sentence interrupted him.

"However" she said, speaking the word with evident pride and following it with a theatrical pause, "We have had a cancellation and there is a single room which you may have for one night".

Gavin Salter smiled the broad smile again, only this time the sentiment behind it was quite genuine. At that moment, feeling the way he did, it was the best possible thing he could have heard.

"Your passport" she said, extending her right hand. He took the passport from the inside pocket of his leather coat and she examined it meticulously before handing it back. Then he picked a ballpoint pen out of its holder and quickly filled in the form she had placed in front of him.

"First floor" she said, passing him a key.

The room was spartan with minimal furnishings and the dark brown carpet was cheap and rough. The plain white bed linen looked worn but clean. He kicked his shoes off, hung his coat on a plastic hanger in the tiny wardrobe and sat on the edge of the bed.

He felt safe in the drab little room, then realised immediately that the feeling might be completely irrational. For all he knew, someone could be on his trail at that very moment. Even so, he sensed that he had put a fair distance between himself and whatever the danger was that he was in, at least for the time being.

Then suddenly he remembered something. Something that was very important to him and which he had been neglecting.

He unzipped the suitcase, searched among his clothes and took out a small book with a soft black cover and coloured ribbon markers. Sitting down again, he opened it at the section marked Night Prayer.

His daily prayers had always been important to him, ever since he had been ordained. Saying the different offices throughout the day was part of what being a priest was about. It kept him going, especially in the difficult times, and made him feel he wasn't doing it all on his own but as part of the Church worldwide. So he felt bad that he'd completely forgotten about it in the rollercoaster of the last thirty-six hours. He crossed himself.

"Whoever dwells in the shelter of the Most High and abides under the shadow of the Almighty ... ". The familiar words of the psalm washed over him.

. . .

Salter put large, thick slices of ham, gruyere cheese and rye bread onto his plate. He reached for the low-fat spread, hesitated, then took two portions of butter. Not the time for worrying about calories, he thought. Then he filled a tumbler with chilled orange juice from the dispenser and poured a cup of strong black coffee from a vacuum jug. Deciding the fresh air would do him good, he carried the tray across the dining room and out onto the patio, sitting down at a small table spread with a stiff white linen table cloth that reached to the ground. For him, breakfast was always one of the luxuries of travelling and as he drank the refreshingly cold orange juice he wondered why he never treated himself to all this when he was at home. All he needed to do was take the time, he thought, and get out of the habit of grabbing leftover pizza from the fridge or cramming a handful of salami between two slices of bread for a quick sandwich. When all this was over and he got back to Hadleigh Bridge, he would start making himself a decent breakfast, Viennese style.

After a blissful night's sleep and a long hot shower, he felt ready to get to grips with what was happening to him and whatever it was he'd become involved in. He tried to empty his mind of all the confusion and anxiety of the previous day. He wouldn't be able to make sense of any of it unless he was totally objective. That was the one thing he could be certain of.

As he ate, his thoughts went back to that afternoon when he'd first met Stefanov Anderek. Now it seemed an eternity away.

What had Anderek wanted? The contact with him was clearly of secondary importance. What he was really interested in was St Mary's Church. He wanted free and unhindered access to it. So he needed the priest not just to give his permission, but also to keep quiet about the whole thing and actually help with the cover up. The story about the triangular stones must have been part of the hoax. Just as the ancient document had been. Clever, he had to admit. Ingenious in fact.

But why? Why was he trying to get a bunch of his cronies into the churchyard so they could nose around and dig it up? What was he really after? There must be something else he knew about that was buried there. Something really valuable. Something worth a fortune. Gold? Diamonds? A haul from a major robbery? Stuff that had been buried there for years?

He took a large mouthful of the coffee. That must be it, he thought. Or something very like it. Right now, he could be involved in an operation worth millions. Whoever these people were, they weren't playing games. And he'd given himself away by doing a runner.

Then suddenly his scepticism kicked in again. Come on, he thought. Can this be real? Who do you think you are? Bloody James Bond? Get a life, for Christ's sake! Why should you be mixed up in something straight out of a detective thriller? Things like that just don't happen. Except in films. There could still be a rational explanation for everything. Anderek could just be a deluded academic. Those characters you met could be a bunch of eccentrics looking for a bit of excitement in their dull and empty lives. It could all be the pipe dream of some mad professor that had gone wrong and got a bit out of hand. Get a grip on yourself!

He ate the last of the cheese and rye bread and finished the coffee. Now, he thought. Look at the immediate options. No harm in that. And try to keep an open mind about everything. He wasn't looking down the barrel of a gun with a silencer on the end of it, at least not yet. And no-one, as far as he was aware, had tried to poison his coffee. If he really was being followed, the best thing he could do was to stay calm and avoid any hasty moves. They'd be expecting him to make a dash for the airport now, so he should stick around Vienna, at least for a day. And if it was all in his imagination and he was really in no danger at all, well, he'd lose nothing by relaxing for a few hours in one of Europe's most beautiful cities. He'd not been to Vienna before, so why not make the best of his first visit?

At reception, he made arrangements to leave his suitcase. The same woman was behind the desk, looking as if she had not moved since the previous night, and with some apprehension, he asked if the hotel could change his Slovakian currency. She stared at him. Then with a long sentence containing the word "however" followed by another theatrical pause, she explained that it was not their normal practice, but that she was prepared to do so in this case. For a moment, he thought he detected the merest of smiles on her face. As he turned and walked away from reception, he picked up a map of the Metro and a glossy leaflet advertising the famous Café Landtmann.

It was a bright, clear day and there was a light breeze. Checking the map again, he headed north along Laxenburger Strasse towards the Südtiroler Platz. At that moment, life was good. He'd almost forgotten the hectic chain of events that had led him there. For now, he was the man of leisure, the comfortably-off traveller who had the time and resources to enjoy what the world had to offer. He slowed his pace down. Why hurry? Take it easy. He didn't have to be anywhere by any time. Today he was his own boss.

Something made him look round.

The traffic was light. A large shiny Mercedes glided by, a man in dark glasses at the wheel. People strolled or hurried to their business. Further back down the street, a youngish man with fair hair, wearing a light blue sweatshirt, stopped where he was in the middle of the pavement, unzipped the canvas bag he was carrying over one shoulder, took out a magazine and opened it.

Salter shook his head thoughtfully and carried on walking. It wasn't far now to the Metro.

. . .

He got off the Metro at Schottentor, walked south along Schottengasse and into Dr Karl Lueger Ring. He was pleased the weather was holding. The blue sky and fluffy clouds looked to be settled in for the day and the air seemed remarkably fresh and clean for the centre of a large city.

Ahead was the imposing frontage of the Café Landtmann, its terrace packed with tables, each one shaded with a red and yellow striped parasol. He'd heard about this place from friends. They'd said it was an experience not to be missed if ever he was in Vienna. So it was time to indulge himself, he reckoned, and sod the expense. And with that thought, he walked through the entrance door and into the main dining room.

A few minutes later, and after a lengthy conversation with a waiter who was clearly keen to try out his English, he was enjoying a steaming hot milky coffee in an enormous cup and a large slice of chocolate cake.

Once again, his mind made a link between food and Catherine Laurence and he thought how much she'd enjoy all this. She'd probably start by saying she didn't want any, then insist on helping herself to a large chunk of his. Why did women always do that? Then she would deliberately leave chocolate around her mouth, pretending not to notice it, until he wiped it off for her with his napkin. Of course if they were alone somewhere, he'd lick it off.

So how was he going to explain to her the situation he'd got into? And how could he make sense of it to her if he couldn't make sense of it himself? He wondered if he could just stick with the lie he'd told her when they'd last seen each other. She'd seen through it, he was pretty certain of that. But when he got back and they were together again, maybe it wouldn't matter so much. He could polish it up a bit. Add a few details and say he'd forgotten them when he told her the first time round. That would make it alright. Then they could just pick up where they left off. More evenings together. More fun. More sex.

But what was he saying? He'd lied to her. And now he was thinking about making the lie even bigger. Just so he could have her around again. Was that really what he wanted? Lies? And then more lies if the lies didn't work?

No, it wasn't. What he wanted was for them to be together, loving and trusting each other. He knew that now. He didn't want anything to come between them. No pretence. No falsehood of any kind. He wanted them to share a life. And that meant being honest about everything, and never holding anything back.

He would just have to tell her what had happened. How he'd got mixed up in something he didn't fully understand. How it all looked so glamorous and exciting. How he'd been drawn into it. And why he'd felt he had to lie to her. He would head back to the hotel now, then sort out a flight to London as soon as he could. Tomorrow he would see Catherine.

He pushed the empty plate away and finished the coffee. It was nearly cold and he wondered how long he'd been sitting there. He looked at his watch. Five to eleven. He gestured to the waiter, who brought the bill, and he paid.

The terrace seemed even busier now and waiters flitted between the tables, skilfully balancing their loaded trays. As he stepped out onto the street, he glanced at the people drinking their teas and coffees. He had always derived great pleasure from watching a crowd of people and imagining things about them. When he had first been to boarding school, he'd played a game in which he pretended he was invisible and could watch what the other boys were doing without them seeing him. Something to do with the loneliness he felt. Maybe this was the same game.

Who was the smooth looking guy in the suit reading the newspaper? A wealthy tycoon planning his next merger? And how about that forty-something woman with the blonde hair and all the jewellery? Had to be a film star. Or could be in the fashion business, here for a meeting with a top designer. That family were American. No doubt about that. Husband, wife and two-point-four children enjoying their first trip to Europe.

And where had he seen him before? The young man with fair hair in a light blue sweatshirt. Sitting with his back to him. With a canvas bag slung over the back of his chair.

Salter was about to walk on in the direction of Schottengasse. Then he stopped.

He'd seen him in the Laxenburger Strasse, just an hour or so before. When he'd sensed that someone was following him, he'd stopped and turned round. The man had stopped as well, and had opened the bag and taken out a magazine and started reading it. Although he'd not been aware of it, Salter's mind had registered that it was an odd thing to do in the middle of the street.

He stared hard at the man's back. The man was sitting completely still. Salter took the Metro map out of his pocket and looked at it, and as he did so he wandered a few paces along the street. He stopped. His view of the man was now partially obscured by one of the large potted shrubs that stood around the edge of the terrace. That was alright, he thought. He didn't want the man to see him watching him. He was alright here for a moment. Just another tourist checking his map.

From where he was now, he had a side view of the man. He was wearing dark glasses. In front of him on the table were a glass and a bottle of mineral water. What now? he thought. Was this paranoia, or was this guy really following him? It could be a complete coincidence that he'd seen him twice in one morning. And even if he was following him, what proof was there that he was connected with Anderek and those others?

He could just be a petty criminal who targeted foreigners

and was looking for the right moment to pick his pocket.

Salter walked a few more paces, slowly this time, looking at the Metro map and occasionally tracing a line with his finger, but all the time watching the man out of the corner of his eye. Not once did the man look up or turn his head.

Decision time, he thought. He folded the map and put it back into the inside pocket of his coat. Then he turned purposefully on his heel and walked south, away from Schottengasse and towards the Vienna Rathaus, now ahead of him in all its architectural splendour.

. . .

Salter crossed the street and headed for the Rathaus Park, walking at a slow and steady pace. He made a point of not stopping or looking around. Within a few minutes, he had skirted the Rathaus itself and was standing in one of the streets behind it.

If the man really was following him, then he'd done a very professional job so far, he thought. He'd certainly managed to keep out of sight on the Metro, and out in the open between Schottentor and the Landtmann. But then Salter hadn't been looking for him. He reckoned now that if he was extra careful, he could outwit him. He looked up and down the street until he spotted a small shop selling craft items and gifts. Perfect, he thought. He turned around casually, pretending to read the street signs. It was quiet, with very little traffic and only a few pedestrians. Was the man watching him? Hiding somewhere? He might find out, and very soon. For now, all he needed to do was stay calm and relaxed.

An electric bell rang softly as Salter opened the shop door and went in. The lighting was subdued and coming in from the brightness outside, his eyes took a brief moment to adjust. Then he noticed the low wooden counter towards the back of the shop and the pretty, fair-haired young woman in a loose cotton dress standing behind it.

"Grüss Gott" he said, remembering just in time the traditional Austrian greeting, always spoken before anything else was said. She gave him a friendly smile and returned the greeting.

"Speak English?" he asked. She nodded.

"That's good" he said. "If it's alright with you, I'll look around. I'm trying to find a gift for someone and I've no idea what to buy".

"Please take your time. Ask me if you need help". She gave him the friendly smile again.

While they had been speaking, he had been keeping one eye on the shop window. Now he walked across the shop to a display of bathroom accessories arranged haphazardly on shelves. Pretending to be interested in an ornate floral-patterned soap dish, he moved a circular chrome mirror until he could see the street outside reflected in it. A couple walked by holding hands. A cyclist rode past. He carried on examining the soap dish.

Angling the mirror again by just a few degrees, he could see the corner of the street he'd come out of five minutes before. He put the soap dish down and picked up a hair brush. He watched. Nothing.

He walked back to the other side of the shop, scanning the items on display to see if he could do the trick with the mirror again. There were no mirrors. He picked up a travelling alarm clock, then put it down again.

"How about a purse or a wallet?" said the woman. "The leather goods are down there".

Salter turned around and followed the direction of her pointing finger. Then he saw the man.

He was still wearing the dark glasses and the canvas bag hung from one shoulder. He had stopped on the other side of the street, diagonally opposite the shop, and he was looking in all directions systematically.

Salter realised he was standing in the light from the window and immediately stepped back.

"Er ... thanks, but that's not really what I'm after. Something else ... perhaps".

The woman shrugged her shoulders. Salter turned his back to the window. Spotting some coffee mugs on a lower shelf, he squatted down. Examining one of the mugs, he shifted his weight from one foot to the other. Then he glanced sideways through the window.

The man was now walking slowly along the street, still on the opposite side from the shop. Briefly, he removed the dark glasses, then put them on again. He's lost me, he doesn't know I'm in here, thought Salter, at the same time praying that it was true. He figured it was dark enough in the shop to prevent the man from seeing him, even though he would have been in his line of vision. He was being careful now to avoid any movements that might attract the man's attention. He put the mug down gently on the shelf and picked up the one next to it, turning it over in his hands. He glanced sideways again. The man walked past and was gone.

Salter stood up, trying to look calm and collected. He had to get out of the shop quickly enough to find out where the man was going, but not so quickly that he would risk the man seeing him. He turned to the young woman.

"I guess my brain's just not in shopping mode today". She laughed. He wasn't entirely sure she had understood the joke.

"Anyway, you've got some lovely things here. Maybe I need time to think about it. I can always come back. I'm staying in Vienna".

She seemed happy with that and gave him another friendly smile. He opened the door and the electric bell rang softly again. He left the shop.

Outside in the street, he looked briefly in the direction the man had gone. He was nowhere to be seen. Salter turned and walked quickly in the opposite direction.

At Schottentor he got onto the Metro again. It was getting busy now that it was nearing lunchtime and that increased the anxiety he was feeling. With all these people around, how could he tell the man wasn't watching him again? He could have doubled back and followed him into the station and onto this very carriage. Just relax, he told himself. He'd gone off in completely the other direction, so he'd have to be bloody fast to have made it onto this train.

Still, he now knew for certain that the man was following him. It wasn't paranoia after all. And in a strange way, he was relieved to discover that. And this man had to be connected with them, whoever they were. There was no other explanation. His mind went back to the thoughts he'd had over breakfast that morning at the hotel. About a cache of gold or jewels buried in the churchyard. About the danger he might be in.

These people must be an organisation of some kind. They couldn't just be a bunch of petty criminals. They must work internationally. Or at least across Europe.

The train had stopped at Karlsplatz. He was so absorbed in his thoughts that he nearly missed the connection. He got off, and as he walked along the platform, he looked over his shoulder for what must have been the tenth time.

By the time he got out again at Südtiroler Platz, he had planned his next move. *This is real secret agent stuff*, he thought with a wry smile. If Catherine knew about this, she'd be making fun of him without mercy. But he reckoned that once again they'd be expecting him to make a dash for the airport and get a plane to England. Instead, he'd get the first train he could to Paris. Then maybe he'd lie low for a day or two. He'd seen how these guys operated and he couldn't afford to take any chances. By now they could have someone waiting in London. Or even in Hadleigh Bridge.

He turned the corner into Laxenburger Strasse. Suddenly he was aware of a commotion. People's voices, talking excitedly. A voice raised above the others, shouting orders. A few yards ahead a crowd had gathered on the pavement, all of them looking down at something. He stopped. The crowd was getting bigger and three or four people in front prevented him from seeing the object of their attention. He squeezed forward. Now there was just one large man blocking his view.

"What's happened?" he whispered to a woman next to him, hoping she understood English.

"Accident" came the hushed reply. "He's hurt. I think dead. No pulse". And she pointed to her neck.

Salter eased himself closer to the large man until he could

see around him. He wasn't prepared for what he saw.

On the ground lay the young man in the light blue sweatshirt. The strap of the canvas bag was round his neck. The bag was half underneath him, as if he had fallen on it. The dark glasses were wrapped around the side of his head at a crazy angle. And from an invisible wound somewhere on his body a pool of blood was spreading across the pavement.

Salter caught his breath as a wave of nausea swept over him. He stood back. The voice he had heard shouted more instructions and from somewhere in the distance came the sound of an ambulance siren.

He turned and walked away in the direction of the hotel.

Chapter 17

Train EC62, bound for Paris via München, pulled out of the Westbahnhof at just after four twenty. Gavin Salter put his leather coat on the luggage rack and settled into the seat. At a restaurant near the station, he'd consumed a veal steak and a litre of beer and felt he could now withstand the fifteen-hour journey.

He looked through the train window. What the hell was going on? And where did he fit into it? None of it made any sense whatever. If that poor bastard's job had been to kill him, how had he managed to get killed himself? Of course, he didn't know for certain the man was dead. But it was pretty likely. The woman had said there was no pulse, so someone in that crowd must have checked for one. And that blood running everywhere. It must have been from a gun or knife wound and he must have died from heavy blood loss. How had that happened in broad daylight, in a busy street? And how had the killer got away?

The beer was making him sleepy and he decided there was no point trying to figure it out. Maybe he would find out later what it was all about. And maybe he wouldn't. And maybe it would be better if he never did. He leaned into the corner of the seat and closed his eyes.

Train EC62 went on through the towns and countryside of northern Austria. Salter read the English newspapers he'd bought at the Westbahnhof and dozed, lightly and uncomfortably. Soon after eight thirty, he changed trains at Münich, with just enough time to get some food from a kiosk. Then his journey continued across Germany, through Strasbourg and into France.

When he'd read all the newspapers, he stared out of the window and thought about himself and his life. It seemed to him there was a kind of inevitability about what had happened over the last few days. It was always on the cards that he would go after something exciting if ever it came along. It wasn't that he was unhappy with what he had. But he was aware that there had always been a restlessness inside him. And the restlessness was born of what he could only describe as emotional claustrophobia. A fear of being tied down. Tied down to one place. Tied to doing one thing. He got a lot out of being the local priest in Hadleigh Bridge. He certainly got job satisfaction, to use the jargon. And he knew that what he did was valued by people. He was successful, if he wanted to use that term. But somehow that wasn't enough. He needed to know that it wasn't the only thing he could have done. Because that had always seemed to him to be tantamount to failure. Doing one thing all your life because it was the only option.

Of course, when he thought about it he knew that was nonsense. It contradicted what he believed in. He'd known people who had committed their lives to doing one thing and doing it well. And in his estimation they were far from being failures. In fact, he'd always looked to them for inspiration and guidance. So if anyone had asked him, he would have said that making a commitment to something and sticking with it was a sign of maturity, a mark of self-confidence. It showed that you knew who you were and what you were all about. The problem was that he couldn't seem to apply that piece of common sense to himself.

And that was why he'd messed things up with Catherine. Catherine had offered him more than anyone else had ever offered him. An easy-going friendship. Accepting and forgiving love. Real happiness. But he'd pushed it all aside to chase after something which had looked glamorous at first, but which had now turned out to be a deception. And a dangerous one at that.

During the early hours, on the last stage of the journey to Paris, he managed to sleep. He was woken by the noise and activity as the train pulled into the Gare de l'Est.

. . .

Another first, thought Salter as he walked out of the station hall and onto the Place 11'me Novembre 1918. He'd never arrived at the Gare de l'Est before. So far he'd always gone Eurostar to the Gare du Nord. He'd been to Paris several times and as he turned into the Boulevard de Magenta and headed south, the memories started coming back. Memories of the bookstalls on the Left Bank and the winding streets of the Latin Quarter and the cramped little restaurants and the churches with their dark interiors. It was coming up to seven thirty now and the streets were getting busy. He liked the feel of the city coming to life around him and as he walked he savoured the atmosphere of it all.

In one of the side streets off the boulevard, he found a small and inexpensive café that was open, and he ordered breakfast. The rich, dark coffee was served in an enormous cup and the taste of the freshly baked bread and the strawberry preserve reawakened his love of French food. As he ate, he decided he would ring Catherine as soon as he'd found somewhere to stay.

. . .

The Hotel Chevalier, with its shoebox rooms and angular furniture, was depressingly modern and totally lacking in the kind of old-fashioned elegance which Salter fondly associated with Paris. But the two women at reception had been friendly and welcoming and when he told them he was spending a few days travelling in Europe and wanted to stay one night with the option of a second, they had smiled encouragingly and handed him a sheaf of glossy brochures.

After unpacking, he shaved and took a shower, then dressed himself in a blue and white striped shirt, light grey linen trousers, brown leather moccasins and a black jacket. The change of clothes felt good after the long journey. He looked at his watch. Nine-thirty. That was eight-thirty in England. Catherine should be leaving for work soon. This would be a good time.

He switched his mobile on, then cursed as the display told him the battery was low. He'd noticed it was low in Bratislava and had meant to charge it then, but he'd completely forgotten about it in his haste to get away. He could charge it now, he thought, but that would take time and he didn't want to risk missing Catherine. Once she'd got to the office, she might be too busy to take a call. He really wanted to straighten things out with her and at least begin to explain what had happened. And in any case, he desperately needed someone to talk to.

He keyed in the code for the UK followed by Catherine's number. It failed to connect and the display repeated its message. With a string of expletives, he threw the mobile onto the bed, where it bounced and landed on the floor.

Picking up the hotel telephone on the bedside cabinet, he followed the instructions on a card and dialled Catherine's landline number. It also failed to connect and there was no sound whatever on the line. Digging his fingernails into the palms of his hands, he tried to take slow, deep breaths. He replaced the handset, waited a few seconds, then called reception. One of the friendly women answered.

"Can you please try and get the following number in England for me" he said, reading off Catherine's number. "I've tried dialling direct from here but I couldn't get through and my mobile needs charging. It's really important. I'd be so grateful".

There was a brief silence.

"I am afraid there is a problem with the lines to the UK at the moment. We have not been able to make any calls there this morning".

"Shit! That's all I fucking need!" he muttered under his breath.

"Pard-*on?*" came the reply.

"I'm ... er ... sorry" he stammered. "What I mean is it's really important I get through to this person today. Can you please try again?"

The woman, sounding very sympathetic, said she would try again and he put the phone down. Then he found the charger for the mobile in his suitcase, plugged it into a wall socket using an adaptor and put the mobile on charge. He locked the room, went down the stairs to reception and left the hotel.

For the rest of the morning and into the afternoon, he walked around Paris. He went north on the Boulevard de Magenta, then west into the Rue La Fayette, past the Opera, into the Boulevard Haussmann and on to the Etoile. Avoiding the noise and traffic of the Champs Elysées, he wandered through a network of streets, most of the time not knowing where he was, until finally the Rue du Faubourg Saint-Honoré took him onto the Rue Royale and the Place de la Madeleine. In the Madeleine itself, he spent a quiet half-hour, staring into the blaze of the votive candles, occasionally praying. Then he walked down Royale to the Place de la Concorde and strolled through the colonnades of the Rue de Rivoli.

Throughout the day, he thought of Catherine. He could feel her walking beside him, holding his hand, her fingers intertwined with his, laughing and making fun of everything, letting him see that she loved being with him. He could see her in every restaurant and café, reaching across the table to take hold of his hand, smiling so beautifully and looking deep into his eyes. And all the time he felt very, very alone. But this time, the being alone was different. Because somehow it didn't feel right.

Around five o'clock, deciding he couldn't walk any more, he took the Metro back to the hotel.

. . .

At the hotel, he went straight to reception. The woman he'd spoken to earlier was standing at the desk, looking strangely as if she had been waiting for him all day. He read her expression before she said anything.

"M'sieur, I am so sorry. I have tried the number in England many times, but there is still a problem. Once I got through and I think I heard a recording on an answerphone but it was a very bad line. I tried to leave a message and I think I was not successful".

He sighed wearily and nodded. "Thank you for trying" he said and walked slowly up the stairs to his room.

He threw his jacket on the bed, walked over to the window and stared out at the buildings opposite. Then he looked at his watch. Five-thirty. God, had he really been out that long. He took the mobile out of the charger and keyed in Catherine's number. He pressed call.

Her phone was switched off, the mechanical voice told him, inviting him to leave a message after the tone. For a moment he hesitated. Then he ended the call.

What made him think she wanted to hear from him again? He'd told her a half-baked pack of lies that she'd seen through immediately. And when he thought things were going his way, before the whole bloody thing went pear-shaped, he hadn't even bothered to contact her. By now she could have found someone else. And who could blame her? He'd really screwed up.

He lay down on the bed. He was tired now and he dozed. After a while, he came round and rubbed his eyes. He checked the time again and it was nearly seven. He got up and went into the bathroom and splashed cold water on his face. Examining himself in the mirror, he decided he was looking old. Then he brushed his teeth and tidied his hair.

Another time, he would have taken a shower and changed at least his shirt. Now he didn't have the motivation to do so. What he needed was to get really drunk. He put his jacket on, picked up the key to the room and closed the door behind him.

After five minutes aimless walking, he found a small restaurant with a cheap and basic menu. He sat near the window, figuring that if he got as drunk as he intended to, the sight of a busy Paris street would prevent him from getting depressed as well. The waiter came with the menu and he ordered a kir.

He settled very quickly on a steak, but he was in no mood to be hurried and he gestured to the waiter and ordered another kir, swallowing the first one down as he did so. Outside the street was buzzing with traffic and people heading home and the restaurant was beginning to fill up. The place must be popular, he thought. Maybe not for an evening-out in style, but certainly as an alternative to cooking.

The waiter hovered and he ordered the steak, specifying medium, and a bottle of Côtes du Rhone. He drank the second kir more slowly, savouring its chill and fragrance. Must make this at home, he thought. Nice drink. Quick and easy.

The waiter appeared again, carrying the steak on an enormous plate with a mountain of fries and salad, and a basket of freshly cut bread. A second waiter brought the wine, pouring a small measure into the glass then standing smartly to attention, holding the bottle in the crook of his arm. Salter sipped the wine. Even through the aftertaste of the kir, he could tell he had made the right choice. It had a well-rounded flavour. And it was strong. He nodded to the man, who filled the glass, bowed politely and disappeared.

The steak was a good inch thick and it was burnt black on the outside, but his knife sliced through the pink flesh as if it were butter and it was one of the most delicious he had ever tasted. The fries were crisp and salty, the salad moist and tangy. The bread was slightly warm with the aroma of yeast. He devoured the meal as if he hadn't eaten for days and by the time his plate was empty, he had drunk two thirds of the wine.

"D'accord, m'sieur? Est-ce que vous voulez du dessert? Ou du fromage?"

Salter had been staring blankly out of the window and hadn't noticed the waiter, who had picked up the bottle and was refilling his glass. He ordered camembert. As the waiter left, he drank a large mouthful of the wine, aware that the alcohol was having the desired effect.

The cheese arrived, a generous portion accompanied by more bread. He cut a large piece. It was ripe and the rich flavour had a bitter edge to it. He emptied his glass, then filled it again with what was left of the wine. Around him, the restaurant was in full swing. Couples and groups of people drank and laughed and talked animatedly. He suddenly noticed he was the only one sitting alone.

He finished the wine and ordered coffee and a large cognac. He knew he was long past the point at which he could hope to wake up in the morning without a hangover, so he might as well do the job properly. He stirred brown sugar into the coffee, then cradled the cognac glass in both hands, swirling the golden liquid around for a few minutes to warm it. Then he swallowed half the contents of the glass, enjoying the burning sensation as it ran down his throat. After a moment's pause, he drank the rest and ordered another one.

A priest friend of his, who had worked in Paris, had once told him that, in spite of their reputation, the French were actually very sparing in their consumption of wine. As he paid the bill and got up unsteadily from the table, he thought his fellow diners must have guessed he was English. Outside in the street, he took a deep breath of the cool evening air and walked slowly back towards the hotel.

Getting drunk hadn't made him happy. It had only anaesthetised him, so that he didn't have to think too deeply about anything. For the moment, he'd forgotten about Catherine. And he'd forgotten about them, the ones who were following him, whoever they were. Now it was just him. Alone.

He switched the light on in the room and closed the curtains. Then he threw his clothes in a heap on the floor and fell into bed. He was asleep within seconds.

Chapter 18

As he'd expected, the hangover was a bad one. In fact, it was the worst kind. The kind that didn't come on till a few seconds after he'd woken up, then hit with full force. He'd had them before, though mercifully not very often. His tongue felt like sandpaper and was stuck to the roof of his mouth. The whole of his head throbbed and needles pierced into the back of his eyes. His body was covered in cold sweat. With some effort, he dragged himself out of bed and into the shower and turned the regulator to hot. For several minutes he stood under the powerful blast, stretching his limbs and massaging the back of his neck. Then after drying himself and getting dressed, he took two of the powerful painkillers he kept for just such occasions.

For a brief moment, he thought of the bottle of scotch in his suitcase and wondered whether a shot of that might take the edge off it. But having so far kept off that slippery slope, he decided he wasn't going to stumble onto it now.

In the breakfast room he poured ice-cold grapefruit juice into a tumbler and filled a large cup with strong black coffee. The painkillers were slowly beginning to work. He swallowed down the juice with difficulty, then sat over the coffee, stirring it and nursing his feelings of regret and self reproach.

The events in Bratislava and Vienna and the man lying in a pool of blood seemed to belong to a different world now. Perhaps they weren't following him any more. Perhaps they never had been. At any rate, he saw no purpose in staying around any longer. He'd lie down for a bit until the headache had gone off, then head for the Gare du Nord and get a seat on Eurostar. Then when he was home and thinking a bit more clearly, he would start putting things back together. If that were possible.

He finished the coffee and got himself another one from the buffet.

. . .

Another glorious morning he thought as he left the Hotel Chevalier wheeling his suitcase behind him. Whatever else had happened on this trip, the weather had certainly been on his side. His mood was lighter than it had been the previous day, when he had walked for hours, and thanks to the painkillers and the black coffee the effects of the hangover were beginning to wear off. Now he felt nostalgic for Paris. He looked at his watch. The Gare du Nord wasn't far away, easy walking distance, even with luggage. He thought he might get a ticket for later that afternoon, then he would have a few hours to play with. He could go to Montmartre and grab a quick lunch at one of those cafés he loved in the Place du Tertre. And he could spend time in Sacre Coeur. That wonderful image inside the dome, of Christ spreading his arms in a great embrace, had always inspired him. And he could use some inspiration right now.

Deciding he needed to get off the main streets, he took a left as soon as he could. Then a right, and a left again. He was lost already, but that didn't matter. He could check out the map he had in his pocket, or ask directions to the station. For now he was where he wanted to be. Small shops and cafés, grey stone buildings, Parisians going about their daily business. He slowed down so he could take it all in.

What was he going to do when he got back? First of all the usual tedious stuff, like check his emails and correspondence. Then ring the churchwardens to tell them he was around again. Then ring Catherine.

Once again he found himself thinking about how he was going to explain it all to Catherine. And he could just hear her saying "Leave it out! You're imagining it all! People like you don't get involved in all that romantic mystery stuff! Get real!" He smiled to himself as he thought of it and decided he'd worry about what to say to her when he got back.

Now that he was feeling a bit better, it was time for something to eat. Maybe even a large café-au-lait. He looked up and down the street. Ahead and on the opposite side there was a café, typically French he thought, with tables outside. And from there he could just make out a selection of pastries in the window. The street was quiet. A small white car some distance away seemed to be slowing down. Parking, he guessed. Or trying to. Must be difficult finding a parking place round here. Bad as London.

He found a gap between the parked cars and stepped into the street. He felt a tug on his arm. The wheel of the suitcase had lodged itself in a crack in the pavement. He pulled at it irritably and it came away. He took a step forward.

The noise of a car engine revving made him look to his left and his blood froze. The small white car he had seen was bearing down on him at speed and in a split second he glimpsed the face of the driver, a man wearing wraparound dark glasses with a black woolen hat pulled down round his ears. His expression was set, the muscles in his neck stood out.

Salter threw himself backwards and the back of his legs felt the wing of a parked car. He kicked his legs into the air and rolled over the car's bonnet, the heel of one of his shoes scraping the white car as it shot past. Putting a hand out to break his fall, he slid off the car and landed on the pavement, his head narrowly missing the curb.

For a moment he lay still. Then slowly he moved his arms and legs and straightened his spine. He wasn't hurt, although his hip felt as if it might be bruised.

An elderly woman appeared, bending over him, babbling incomprehensibly and smoothing his hair with her hand. A man in a cloth cap and overalls was gesticulating wildly in the direction the white car had gone and talking in guttural tones. A small crowd was gathering.

Salter got to his feet, the woman carefully helping him. He stood up straight and clasped her hand warmly.

"Merci, merci. D'accord, d'accord" he said, pointing to himself to indicate he was unhurt. The woman seemed satisfied with this demonstration and with a sweet smile and further incomprehensible words of kindness and encouragement, accompanied by a forceful stab of the finger, she went on her way. The man in overalls meanwhile muttered something and made one final gesticulation, then nodded reassuringly to Salter and walked off. The small crowd melted away as quickly as it had formed.

Salter crossed the street. Whatever it was that was happening, to him or around him, it was now far beyond any coincidence. The driver of that car had been following him and had meant to run him down and kill him. And he'd failed to do so purely by chance. The man in Vienna had the same thing in mind, except he'd ended up as a corpse. How was he planning to do it, he wondered. Gun? Knife? Poison of some kind? Either way, they were on his trail right across Europe. And if they were prepared to go to that much trouble, then they probably wouldn't stop until he was dead. He shivered at the thought of that. It was unreal. But at the same time, horribly real.

Where was he going to be safe? There was no way of knowing. The guy in the car wouldn't be back. Too risky to try it again. So he was probably alright where he was, at least for a while. Their next attempt would be somewhere else. Maybe at the station. Or even on the train. Maybe even in London.

He would have to go to the police as soon as he got back to England, however ridiculous his story sounded. At least they could give him protection. They'd probably think he was mad and lock him up.

He sat down at a table inside the café and ordered the café-au-lait he'd promised himself. And suddenly feeling ravenously hungry, he ordered a pastry. Making a concerted effort to relax, he consumed the food and drink with enjoyment.

There was no point wasting any time now, he thought. He had no way of knowing what would happen next or where it would happen, and if he spent any longer sightseeing, it could be his last trip to Paris. It was down to getting to the station, and quickly. He took the map out of his pocket, found where he was and worked out the shortest route to the Gare du Nord. Then he paid the bill and left the café.

He turned left and hoped he was going the right way. Direction finding had never been one of his skills. In fact he'd always felt himself to be utterly useless in that respect and dreaded being in strange places on his own. Within only a few yards of the café, he'd stopped to look at the map again. He wasn't certain that he shouldn't be going in completely the opposite direction and for a moment he turned around and looked back the way he'd just come.

As he turned, a figure ducked into a doorway and his eye caught a flash of red on blue.

Salter stood completely still, staring in the direction in which he'd seen the figure. So, he thought, these bastards really are organised. They fail once and they're ready to try again within minutes. The doorway the man had disappeared into was in shadow and he strained his eyes for the slightest sign of movement. Whoever it was that wanted him dead, he was determined they weren't going to find it easy.

He walked slowly on. His mysterious friend was on the same side of the street as he was, so he'd stay with it. He stopped again and made as if to turn round, but didn't. Let's get him nervous, he thought. Then he's more likely to make a mistake. He walked on again. He guessed this one planned to use something like a knife and then make it look like a street robbery by stealing his wallet or slashing the suitcase open.

He stopped, and this time he did turn round with a swift movement. The figure also moved quickly, but not quickly enough, allowing Salter to see that the flash of red was a scarf or bandana tied around the neck and the blue a shirt or jacket, before the figure ducked down behind a parked car. He also caught sight of a hat of some kind, possibly a baseball cap, with the brim pulled well down over the forehead. Now that wasn't very clever, thought Salter. He's obviously rattled, or at least off his guard, hiding behind a car like that. Not much cover and drawing attention to himself as well. So far, so good. He walked on.

Despite his new found confidence, he had to admit to himself that he didn't know what he was going to do next. He had no weapon to use, not even an improvised one, and therefore no effective means of defending himself against someone who was in all probability a violent thug, if not a trained assassin. Running for it didn't seem an option. Although he was healthy, he wasn't very fit. And in any case, he could well be up against someone who knew the streets of Paris better than he did and could easily catch up with him or cut him off before he got very far. His only chance of survival was to outwit him. And it was a slim chance. Maybe this was Judgment Day for him. Maybe he was about to be dispatched to meet this God he'd preached to other people about so often.

Then a miracle happened.

On his right he saw a narrow, dark alleyway which looked like a service entrance to the shops. At the same time, he noticed that he could see clear reflected images in some of the shop windows on the opposite side. And a strategy for getting out of this mess alive suddenly raced through his brain. He stopped and turned around again. The phantom stalker was nowhere to be seen. He stood for a moment, looking back down the street. A few people walked past. But no sign of the man in red and blue. Maybe he was still crouched behind the car. Hopefully getting cramp in his legs. He waited. Then he dived into the alleyway, pushing the suitcase in front of him.

At first he stood with his back to the wall, his body tensed. Then slowly he relaxed. No point in stiffening up, he thought. That wouldn't help. He faced in the direction he'd just come from, at the same time keeping an eye on the shop windows across the street.

Everything would depend on how fast he could move. He'd have to rely on the reflections in the windows to gauge when the man was getting close. Then when he got to the opening of the alleyway, he would grab him and drag him in. And then it would be a question of inflicting serious injury as quickly as he possibly could, so that the man was at least temporarily disabled. He could use one of the self-defence tricks he'd learned in the cadet force at school, like two-fingers-in-the-eyes. Or he could head-butt him full in the face and break his nose, followed by a knee in the groin. Then he could finish by cracking his head against the wall, which was pretty sure to knock him out.

For a brief moment he was shocked at his own coldness and calculation, as he systematically planned this horrific damage to a fellow human being. He was a priest, for Christ's sake!

But then he knew that if he hesitated for a second, this stranger would do even worse things to him. Everything depended on him getting in there first.

He looked across the street at the shop windows. There reflected was the figure, walking slowly and deliberately, with about twenty yards to go, he guessed, before he came level with the entrance to the alleyway. He flexed his fingers and the muscles in his arms. His heart pounded inside his chest. His lungs threatened to burst with the force of his controlled breathing. Close to the alleyway a grey Citroen van was parked.

He saw its image in one of the shop windows and he knew that when the figure passed behind it, he would be just feet from where Salter was standing.

He moved across to the opposite wall of the alleyway to give himself better cover, but kept his eyes fixed on the shop window. Now the figure was there in the window. And it passed behind the van.

Gavin Salter reached out into the street with both hands, grabbed hold of the figure by the clothing on its chest and pulled it into the alleyway, flinging it against the wall.

"Take this, you bastard!" he shouted with all the force he could summon up. His hand grasped the end of the red bandana, a button flew off the blue shirt and the baseball cap fell to the ground.

And he found himself looking into the terrified face of Catherine Laurence.

Chapter 19

Gavin Salter fell back against the wall and his arms dropped limply to his sides. For what seemed ages, they stared at each other.

"What the hell are you doing here?" he said, barely able to get the words out. "And how did you know where I was?"

"The hotel" said Catherine, wiping her nose with the back of one finger. "They left a message on my answerphone. There was some problem with the line and it crackled a lot, but I got just enough of it. They said their name and your name too. After that, it wasn't hard to trace them on the Internet. And my boss owed me a favour so I asked for a couple of days off. I had to wait around for a ticket on Eurostar and I didn't get to the Gare du Nord till the early hours. Then I dossed there for a while until some gendarme started hassling me. I went looking for your hotel first thing this morning".

"So you've been following me?"

She nodded. "Since you left the hotel. I just couldn't make any sense of things. You told me all that stuff about going up north and I knew it was crap, so you had to be somewhere else. When I realised where you'd ended up, I thought you must be in trouble of some kind. I figured if you'd just skipped off to

Paris to screw someone, you wouldn't be getting the hotel to ring me up and tell me about it. And that's when I decided to get out here and find out what was going on".

Salter nodded slowly as he took in what she was saying. He felt reality gradually seeping back into this nightmare situation.

A man and woman peered into the alleyway, clearly worried about the violence they'd just witnessed. Then they glared and walked off. A woman passed by and glanced at Catherine, muttering something. Salter tried to think of something to say to them by way of explanation, but couldn't think of anything. He looked at Catherine again.

"So why didn't you just let me know you were here?"

"I didn't know how you'd take it. Like I said, I had no idea what you'd got yourself into and I was worried I might make things worse if I just grabbed you in the street. So I reckoned I'd wait and see what happened next. And then I saw that thing with the white car and it really spooked me. Was that just a lousy driver or has someone got it in for you big time?"

Salter rested his head on the wall behind him and let out a deep breath.

"I've got myself involved in something but I don't know what it is. There are people trying to kill me. I'm pretty certain of that now. I wasn't sure until that guy tried to run me down. I reckon it's just been luck that they haven't succeeded. And if I hang around much longer, the luck's going to run out".

"So I suppose you thought I was one of them, whoever they are".

"Yeah, I did. Sorry about the rough stuff".

"Listen," said Catherine, "how about we go somewhere quiet

and get a drink, and you can tell me all about this. Or at least what you know of it".

"That sounds good. Then we can think about getting home".

Catherine looked at him. Then she reached out and took hold of his hand.

"Is that really such a good idea? These people must have seen you've got luggage, so they'll be expecting you to go straight from here to the Gare du Nord. For all you know, one of them could be there right now. Why not stay another night and travel tomorrow? That might throw them off the scent for a while".

"Right. That makes sense. I'm just not thinking straight. I'll find a hotel and stay another night".

Catherine looked at the ground.

"And what do you want to do with me?"

Salter squeezed her hand.

"Stay with me. Please" he said.

. . .

Catherine sat down on the edge of the bed and kicked off her trainers. Then she took her socks off and screwed them into a tight ball.

"I wouldn't get too near those if I were you" she said, throwing them across the room.

Salter was unzipping his suitcase and removing some of the contents. They had spent the last hour sitting over several cups of black coffee in the back of a small dark café. He had told her about Anderek and the ancient document, about Slovakia and what had happened to raise his suspicions, about the strange series of events in Vienna. And he had told her why he had lied to her. She had held his hand and patiently listened to it all. Then they had booked a room in the first hotel they could find.

"Have you got a change?" he said, hanging jackets and trousers in the wardrobe.

"Yes, I've got a dress and some decent shoes in there" she said, pointing to the small black canvas haversack lying in the middle of the bed. Until then, he'd hardly noticed she was carrying it.

Catherine untied the red bandana, shook it out, then tossed it onto the floor. Opening the neck of the haversack, she delved into it with both hands. Finding a toothbrush and paste, she went into the bathroom and turned the basin tap on.

"Not bad for a cheap hotel" she called out. "Quite a large bathroom, really. And pretty clean".

He listened to the sound of her brushing her teeth as he hung his leather coat over the back of a chair. She came back into the room, wiping her mouth on a towel.

"How do you feel about ... ?" He stumbled over the words.

"Getting in bed with you? I might consider it. Even though you're a lying bastard".

She unbuttoned the denim shirt, slipped it off her arms and let it fall. Then she unzipped her jeans and stepped out of them. She was wearing nothing now except for a pair of white lace knickers. For a moment she looked into his eyes. Then she slid the knickers down her legs and pushed them away with her foot. She walked across the room to where he was standing and pressed herself against him. Her arms closed around his neck

and he felt the tip of her tongue on his cheek.
"Guess what" she said, softly biting his ear lobe.
"What?" he whispered back
"I haven't showered since yesterday morning".

Chapter 20

The bright, spacious office was situated in one of the city's newest and biggest blocks and the large, plate-glass window provided a spectacular view of Lake Geneva. Today the sky was blue and crystal clear, so the view was even better than usual.

The man was aged about sixty and had a full head of snow white hair that grew thick around his ears and on the back of his neck. His face was deeply tanned, which gave the skin a leathery appearance and a network of lines showed at the corner of his eyes and around his mouth. He was dressed in a blue pinstripe suit and cream silk shirt, and the black knitted tie was held in place by an ostentatious gold clip. The lenses of his heavy horn rim spectacles were rose-tinted.

He struck a match and lit a large Havana cigar, slowly and with great care. He never hurried when he lit one of his favourite cigars. It was something to take time over. Like looking at the view, which he did several times a day. He loved the view of the lake.

"We got rid of that moron who played Janovic".

He spoke in English with a heavy Swiss German accent and the tone was resonant and menacing. He drew on the cigar and inhaled luxuriously. Then he swivelled the black leather chair round to face the man who was sitting on the other side of the large mahogany desk.

"We have no use for people who make stupid mistakes. We simply cannot tolerate them. In any case, he was just a criminal thug. We can recruit his kind any time we need them".

He put the cigar into a white marble ashtray. Then for several seconds he stared at the man opposite him. The man shifted uncomfortably in his chair.

"Of course, you understand I was hoping to hear better news by now. I was expecting to be told that this priest had been eliminated. I wanted to hear he'd suffered an unfortunate accident and that consequently there was no danger of him talking to anyone, especially the police. Instead I hear he is not only alive and well but safely on his way back to England".

He paused to pick up the cigar.

"So tell me, what went wrong in Vienna?"

The man who called himself Stefanov Anderek took a deep breath, working hard to maintain his composure. He knew he was in a lot of trouble. His life could even be in danger.

"I'm afraid we don't know. We put Lichvar on the job but he was killed before he had a chance to do anything and we couldn't find out who'd done it. We think it must have been a street robbery that went wrong".

The man stared again, silently. There was something about that stare from behind the rose-tinted lenses that even Anderek found intimidating.

"That isn't good enough" said the man, speaking the words slowly and deliberately. "In this organisation we need to know everything". He drew on the cigar.

"And what about Paris? Do you have a plausible excuse for that?" The voice was full of sarcasm.

"There's only ever one chance with a hit-and-run. He saw it coming and he was just too quick. The car was stolen, of course. It's been disposed of and there's no way the police can trace it back to us".

The man laughed. It was a rasping, metallic sound, with no humour in it.

"I should hope not, for your sake" he said, putting the cigar down again and folding his hands on the desk in front of him. "We can't afford to get it wrong in our line of work. It puts everything at risk. And in any case I shouldn't have to be telling you these things. You know our organisation and how it runs. You've been with us for long enough".

Anderek looked at the floor. He was dying for a cigarette but didn't want to push his luck by asking if he could smoke.

"So what happens now?" said the man, leaning back in the leather chair.

"We use the alternative strategy" said Anderek. "We'll have to put the operation back now by about two weeks. After what's happened, we can't afford to take any risks whatever. But apart from that, it will all go ahead as planned".

"And the priest? What about him?"

"We've been watching the Gare du Nord since this morning. We'll get him before he gets on the train. Poisoned needle".

The man nodded slowly.

"I want you to take personal charge of the operation from now on. Be in London when it all happens". Another pause and the silent stare.

"And don't let anything else go wrong".

He struck a match and relit the cigar, then swivelled the chair round to face the window. Anderek got up and left the room, closing the door quietly behind him.

As he looked out of the window at the city and the lake beyond, he wondered if he'd been a bit harsh. After all, the man who now called himself Stefanov Anderek was one of their best men. He was single-minded, professional and completely ruthless. These were only small hitches. He would finish the job in spite of them. No question of that.

He smoked the cigar and thought how much he loved the view.

Chapter 21

Through the window of the hotel room the sky could just be seen above the buildings opposite. It was early evening now and would soon be dusk.

Gavin Salter lay in bed with his arm around Catherine. Her head rested on his shoulder. She was asleep. For hours they had made love with unrestrained passion, then rested, then loved again, their bodies seeming to melt together as they climaxed.

He had told her how he felt about her, and how he had realised that he was in love with her. And she had said that she was in love with him. And then they had made love again, and he had felt cleansed of all his guilt.

Now he drew her gently towards him and kissed her lips, running his tongue along her teeth. She stirred. Her eyes flickered open, gradually focussing. She smiled.

"Don't tell me you want to do it again!"

"Shut up" he said, throwing the duvet back and slapping his hand on her bare thigh. "It's time to think about food and drink. You realise we're in Paris, even if we didn't mean to be. And I guess you haven't eaten much if you got here first thing this morning".

She shook her head, then nuzzled into his shoulder. "I made

sandwiches and ate them on the train, but apart from that I haven't had a thing. And I'm starving".

"That's settled then". He rolled off the bed, lifted her gently to her feet and led her by the hand into the bathroom.

They stood under the shower, their tongues exploring the recesses of each other's mouth as the hot water cascaded over them. He washed her from head to foot and gently rubbed shampoo into her hair. Then they dried each other slowly with thick, fluffy towels.

From the haversack, Catherine produced a neatly folded cotton dress, gipsy-looking with a red, blue and green floral pattern. She pulled it on over her head and slipped her bare feet into black espadrilles. On her left wrist she put a random collection of silver bangles. Her hair had been dried only with a towel and she didn't put any makeup on her face. Salter watched her and thought she looked more beautiful and more desirable than ever. Then he dressed himself in a pink shirt, black jacket and chinos.

Their hotel was close to the Gare du Nord and they soon found somewhere to eat. The small restaurant was everything they could have wanted. The tables and chairs were old-fashioned, solid and basic, the décor tastefully traditional. The heavily starched table cloths gleamed. "M'sieur, madame" said the waiter mechanically as he pulled their chairs out from the table and they sat down.

"Full works tonight, don't you reckon?" said Catherine, biting her lower lip and concentrating on the menu.

"Sorry?"

"Three courses, I mean. And no watching the waistline. Like you said, we're in Paris. I hope you've got your credit card, by the way. This outfit's completely girly, in case you hadn't noticed".

"What?"

"No pockets".

"Oh, I understand. Don't worry. The evening's on me".

"Just like the afternoon". She grinned at him over the top of the menu.

He raised the middle finger of his right hand. She saw it and giggled.

The pâté was coarse, rich and laced with brandy, and the Côtes du Roussillon was a perfect partner to it. They talked and ate and drank and enjoyed being together, and soon the Côtes du Roussillon was finished. Catherine watched with fascination as the veal flambé she had ordered was prepared in front of her, flames leaping dangerously into the air, the juices of the meat spattering in the pan. Salter's grilled lamb arrived decorated with freshly cut herbs. They ordered another bottle of the Côtes du Roussillon.

The main courses were delicious, delicately flavoured and typically French. Catherine talked animatedly, occasionally apologising for speaking with her mouth full. They filled and refilled their glasses with the strong red wine and emptied the second bottle as they finished eating. The attentive waiter removed their plates and glasses and presented them once again with the menu. After a few moments consideration, they both ordered dessert.

As the empty plates were taken away, Catherine leaned on one arm. She looked sleepily across the table and mouthed the words I love you and he felt her bare feet nestling around his ankles.

"Coffee?" he said, reaching out and stroking her cheek with the tips of his fingers.

"Mmmm. Good idea. Might wake me up a bit".

He gestured to the waiter. She closed her eyes for a few seconds, then opened them and sat up straight. She pushed back the cuff of his shirt with one finger and looked at his watch.

"It's too early to go back yet. Let's find somewhere else and get another drink".

"If you like. But shouldn't you be getting some sleep tonight?"

She rubbed her eyes.

"I am tired. I probably look like it too. Sorry. I just don't want to miss out on anything while we've got time together".

Salter took hold of her hand. "You look great. I'm just worried about how you'll feel tomorrow when we travel home. Anyway, we can lie in bed for a while. I'll have breakfast sent up and we can take our time over it".

Catherine stared at him through half-closed eyes and blew a kiss. The waiter brought the coffee.

She was slightly unsteady as they got up from the table. Outside the night air was cool and Salter felt it clear his head. She slipped her arms around his waist and they kissed. Then they walked on down the street holding hands, their fingers intertwined.

"How about that one?" said Catherine, pointing. "Doesn't that look really romantic? And it's warm enough to sit outside". She leaned against him and rubbed her hair into his face.

Gavin Salter followed her pointing finger and saw a brightly lit café with tables on the pavement outside. They sat down. A young woman with a notepad and pen, wearing a white blouse and black skirt, hovered over them.

"Calvados, please" said Catherine.

"Cognac for me" said Gavin Salter. The young woman disappeared into the café.

"I've always loved Calvados. Makes me think of France and all things French". She leaned back in the chair and her head lolled.

"Take it easy. We've both sunk a fair bit and you don't want a hangover like I had this morning".

"So what were you doing last night?" she said, slurring the words slightly.

"Feeling bad about things. And trying to forget whatever it was I was feeling bad about".

"That makes sense. So I guess it must have worked if you were hung over".

"Depends how you measure success, I suppose". The drinks arrived.

Catherine leaned her chin on one hand. "Here's to us" she said, and drank half the contents of the glass. Gavin Salter sipped the cognac.

"So what do you reckon on doing when you get back to England?" Catherine was half slumped over the table now and holding the glass unsteadily to her lips.

"My job, I guess. I'll pick it up again from where I left off. What else is there for me to do?"

"So, you're going to carry on being a clergy-man after all this excitement?" She drank some more of the Calvados.

"I'm not sure it's the kind of excitement anyone needs. I've got involved in something I shouldn't have got involved in and

I still don't know what it's all about. Hadleigh Bridge is quite an attractive prospect after what I've been through in the last few days".

Catherine nodded, slowly and sleepily. She drained the glass.

"And what about us?"

"What do you mean by that? I've told you how I feel. I've told you everything. I love you and I want to be with you always. And unless I've got it completely wrong, I reckon that's what you want too. So whatever happens, we can work something out. Neither of us has any ties. We're in control of our own lives. We can decide for ourselves what we want and it's no-one else's business".

"Yeah, right. But what I'm saying is … "

Catherine had leaned her whole weight on one elbow when the elbow slipped off the edge of the table. She managed to regain her balance before she fell off the chair. The empty glass toppled onto its side and rolled in an arc and Salter just managed to catch it in time.

"Are you sure you're alright?" he said, clutching her hand.

"I'm fine" she said with a grin. "I'm tired but I'm enjoying myself. Anyway, I've got you to look after me, haven't I?"

He felt her bare foot rubbing against his leg. The young woman in the white blouse and black skirt passed by the table. Catherine reached out and touched her arm.

"A cognac, please". She looked at Salter. "How about you?" He nodded. "Make that *deux, s'il vous plait*".

The young woman disappeared again.

"Now, where were we?" She screwed her eyes up, then opened them wide and smiled the beautiful smile. "Ah, yes.

Back home in Blighty. So how are you going to explain me to the parish? Unless of course you were thinking I'd be your secret woman. And you can stuff that for a start".

The two cognacs arrived.

Salter looked serious. "That wasn't what I was thinking at all. You're worth more than that to me".

"Only joking". She squeezed his hand. "I know we have to be discreet. I wouldn't expect it to be otherwise".

Salter looked at her. Her face was flushed from the alcohol, her hair was a mess and the dress had slipped off one shoulder. But in that moment, he thought she was the most beautiful thing he had ever seen or could ever imagine seeing. And he wanted nothing else but her.

"Like I said, we'll sort something out. I'm not the first priest who's had a bit on the ... "

He paused and caught his breath.

"That sounds awful. I'm really sorry. I didn't mean it to ... "

Catherine burst into near hysterical laughter.

"Now that's really honest. That I can live with. No bullshit". She raised the glass of cognac.

"Here's to honesty". And she tipped most of the liquid down her throat.

Salter lifted his glass and took a large sip.

"Alright, I get the message. From now on I have to be honest with you. About everything".

"You got it in one" she said, and drank the rest of the cognac.

"Tell me. Why do people get married?" She was slurring her

words again. "I mean, so many of them are unhappy and the divorce rate's going up and up".

"Yeah, you're right, it is. But I guess people still want to make some kind of commitment to each other. And however much divorce there is, everyone thinks their own marriage is going to be different".

"But you can make a commitment without all this corny stuff in church. I mean, it's all so bourgeois and sentimental. And when it goes wrong, there's all this legal thing to go through. And then people end up doing damage to themselves and each other. Why can't you just be with the person you want to be with? And if it works out, fine. You can stay together for the rest of your life. That gives you a choice. And if it doesn't work out, you separate and there's no harm done".

Salter nodded, frowning slightly. Catherine continued.

"What I mean is, how many of these people who get married in church really care about the religious bit? It's just conformity, isn't it? Walking down the aisle. They'll have affairs and get divorced like anyone else".

"Sure. That's exactly how it is with some people. But there are others who do take it seriously. And if you've got faith and you believe in God, then you'll want God to be in your life. That's what marriage in church is all about. Or rather it should be. That's what we mean by saying marriage is a sacrament".

Catherine leaned her chin on both hands and looked at him. He could see she was finding it difficult to focus.

"So if we're going to be together, you'll be expecting me to get married".

Salter folded his arms and rested them on the edge of the table.

"I think we need time to think about that one".

"And I think we need another drink" said Catherine, and she looked around and raised a hand.

"I'm okay with this one" he said as the young woman came to the table.

"Just for me then. I'll have a large cognac".

The young woman looked at Catherine as she turned and walked away and the disapproval in her eyes was unmistakeable.

Catherine ran her finger down his forearm and over the back of his hand. Her head drooped slightly to one side.

"I guess I could do worse than be married to you. I just worry about this vicar's-wife bit".

Salter took her hand in both of his. Then he lifted her hand to his lips and kissed her fingers.

"Do I detect a stereotype here?" he said, raising his eyebrows. "A vicar's wife is the last thing I need, whatever that means anyway. If we did decide to get married, you'd be married to me, not to my job. Get it into your head, it's you I want, not some imaginary version of you. And I realise now that you're the only person who could really make me happy. I don't know why I couldn't see that before".

A sudden gentle breeze blew strands of hair across her face. She smiled at him, her eyes half-closed, her head once again drooping to one side.

"That all sounds good to me. I'll go for it". She was clearly having difficulty with the words.

The young woman placed the cognac on the table. Salter noticed that the measure almost filled the small balloon-shaped glass. Catherine picked it up and drank a mouthful.

Then she held the glass up close to her face and peered at it, as if something about it suddenly fascinated her.

"Sure you won't have some of this?"

He shook his head. "I think we should be heading back soon. We both need sleep".

"You mean we need bed" she said, emptying the glass in one. Salter signalled to the young woman and she brought the bill. He paid with cash. Catherine was leaning her head on one hand. Her eyes were closed.

As they stood up, she fell against him and he steadied her. Then she slipped her hand round the back of his neck and pulled his head down, pressing her lips against his. Her tongue slid into his mouth and he tasted cognac.

"Sorry, Father. I should wait till we get in the room" she said, putting her head on his shoulder. "Don't mean to embarrass you".

They walked slowly back in the direction of the hotel, stopping occasionally to kiss. The air was warm and the sounds of Paris were all around them.

After what seemed like hours, they arrived at the hotel and took the lift to their floor. In the room, Catherine kicked off the black espadrilles and dropped the silver bangles onto the carpet, where they landed with a soft clatter. Then she slipped the dress over her head and removed her underwear, tossing them both onto a chair. She pushed the hair back off her face, squinted at him and grinned.

"Do you know, you look even sexier after a few drinks" she said, and put her arms around his waist, nuzzling her face into his chest. He felt her warm breath through his shirt.

He gently disengaged her arms and kissed her forehead. "Just let me get undressed. I'll be with you in a minute". He turned away, and out of the corner of his eye he saw her collapse onto the bed and stretch her limbs.

He unbuttoned his shirt and took it off, then put his wristwatch on the dressing table.

"Gavin" said a husky and barely audible voice from behind.

"What is it, darling?" he said, unlacing his shoes.

"I think I'm going to be sick".

Chapter 22

The man took the top off the polystyrene cup and sipped the black coffee. It was hot and it burnt his tongue. *"Merde"* he muttered under his breath. He snapped the top back on and put the cup on the bench next to him, placing it carefully so that it didn't tip over. Then he shifted uncomfortably, stretching first his right leg then his left. Fuck this bloody seat, he thought. Why did the benches at railway stations always have to be so hard? He looked at his watch. Ten past nine. He'd been sitting here for two hours now and it would be nearly another hour before the replacement came to take over. He slipped his hand into his jacket pocket and fingered the plastic tube that held the needle. All he wanted was for this bastard to show so that he could get it over with.

He wasn't supposed to know anything about all this. He and another one had just been told to watch the Gare du Nord in three-hour shifts. But in fact he did know a bit about it. Back at the club that fronted as the organisation's safe house, the guys had been talking. It was always dangerous to talk. They all knew that. Because if they found out you'd been talking, you'd end up in the river with concrete boots on and your throat cut. But they'd been talking anyway because the word was this was a big one and they just couldn't resist talking about it. It was all to do with that Slovakian with the bald head and the moustache. The one who wore all those expensive clothes and the flashy Rolex. The other guys sure envied him. They'd picked up that he was someone really important who went all over the world for the organisation. They all wanted to be like him.

The action was going to be in London, and it was going to be soon. And the man he was now looking out for had somehow managed to blow the cover. So he had to be rubbed out and quick, before he had a chance to get on the train. He had no idea who this man was. All he had was a couple of pictures sent to his mobile. The Slovakian had somehow managed to take them while the man wasn't looking. He must have the same mobile and it was a pretty neat one. The organisation gave them to all their people these days. One of the pictures was really clear and close-up, so he'd have no problem identifying him.

And then it would be in for the kill and he'd have to get it right first time. He'd walk in front of him, bump into him, drop the newspaper he'd bought for the purpose and make a big thing of apologising. Then he'd bend over to pick the paper up and put the needle into the man's ankle. That way there'd be no trace and it would look like a heart attack. This new stuff they were using was really quick-acting. Chances were it would take effect before he realised anything was wrong. He might not even get to the ticket office. He certainly wouldn't make it to the train.

Where was that cunt, he thought as he shifted himself again. He was tired and this whole damn thing was really getting to him. He couldn't feel his backside at all. He was beginning to hate this geezer, whoever he was. He was really going to enjoy killing him. The bastard deserved it for keeping him sitting all that time on the hard seat. He fingered the needle a second time and savoured the thought of what he was going to do.

Of course, he could expect to do alright out of this, so he shouldn't really be complaining. If the job was done, he and the team would be paid well. And the one who'd put the needle in would get a bonus. So if that was him, he'd have a bit of extra cash in his pocket. And then he could have a couple of evenings at that bar he liked. The one where they had the really nice girls. And where you could pay a bit more and get a young one. For a man of his age, that was really something to look forward to.

He tried the coffee again. It was cooler now and he drank several mouthfuls. He'd had nothing to eat since lunch and he was beginning to feel hungry. But of course he couldn't go anywhere now and get food because if he did, the target might show up and he'd miss him. Then he'd be the one who was dead. So food would have to wait, even if it meant eating really late. He'd get something in that café round the corner from the flat, the one that stayed open. That was the way he lived anyway. Living alone with no-one but himself to worry about, he was used to it.

A figure moved into his field of vision. He tensed, then relaxed again. That couldn't possibly be him. This man was thin with blonde hair cut very short and wore a light-grey suit. The man in the pictures was quite broad-shouldered with a thick head of dark hair and was likely to be wearing jeans and a leather coat. He picked up the coffee and drank the remainder of it. The man in the light-grey suit opened a copy of Paris Match and stood where he was, reading it.

He looked at his watch again. Christ, it was twenty past nine. He leaned back, sighed and crossed his legs.

A large man sat down on the bench next to him. He turned his head to look at his new companion and felt the cold of metal against his right wrist. He looked down. His right hand was handcuffed.

His jaw dropped. *"Quoi? Mais qu'est-ce que c'est...?"*

He felt cold metal against his other wrist. He looked round. A second man was standing over him. He was handcuffed between them.

The two men lifted him from the bench and marched him away. The blonde-haired man in the light-grey suit folded his copy of Paris match and led them to a waiting car.

Chapter 23

Gavin Salter keyed a number into his mobile and looked across the room at Catherine asleep in the bed, her hair tangled around her face. One corner of the duvet was pushed back to reveal a bare leg.

By half dragging and half carrying her into the bathroom, he'd managed to get her head over the toilet bowl a split second before she was violently sick. The application of a wet towel to her face had brought her round sufficiently to get her back into bed and then she had passed out. Now, at a few minutes before nine, she was still sleeping soundly.

"Bill Hoxton" said a familiar voice.

"Hi Bill, it's Gavin. How are things at home?"

"A fat lot you care, you lazy bastard, living it up in Europe. So what's the temperature in Slovakia? Or are you too busy skiing and knocking back the vodka to notice?"

"Actually I'm in Paris".

"Oh my God, it's worse than I thought! How did you end up there? Or is that a perk of some kind?"

"Well, it's a long story, as they say in the movies. But right now I need another favour. I plan to head home today. But just in case anything goes wrong and I don't make it for some reason, could you handle things tomorrow? It's all quite straight forward. Just the main service at St Mary's. St John's and St Peter's don't have one this week. And if you'd like to give one of the churchwardens a ring, they can get everything set up for you. I'm sure you could blow the dust off an old sermon".

There was silence. Then Gavin Salter heard a deep, low chuckle.

"Alright, out with it. Who are you shagging this time?"

"Trust you to think of that. I can't go into details at the moment. I'll tell you some time. But how about it? Can you help?"

"Yeah I guess you can count on me, fool that I am".

"Thanks Bill. I won't forget this".

"You bet you won't! This'll mean at least an evening round at your place and a bottle of single malt".

"You got it".

"So, what about this one? Is it serious for a change?"

"Like I said, I'll tell you some time".

"Whatever. But maybe it's time to stop playing the field. None of us are getting any younger. I know it's different for me, I'm gay. But you need to find yourself a good woman. No, forget that. Find yourself a bad one. Then think about settling down. You know, someone to come home to and all that. Who knows, they might even promote you".

"You always were a great one for good advice. I'll certainly think about it".

"So, if I don't hear from you again, I'll be in the saddle tomorrow. Sorry, that wasn't meant to be a joke. Anyway, give my amour to Paris".

"Cheers Bill. And thanks".

He put the mobile down on the dressing table and looked again at Catherine. She was still fast asleep and hadn't moved since he last looked. It was a pity to have to wake her, he thought. She needed that sleep. But they had to get moving and be on their way back to England.

Suddenly he thought of Vienna, and the stranger who had been following him lying dead in the street in a pool of blood. And the car that had come out of nowhere yesterday and tried to run him down. What else were they going to throw at him? And how could he keep Catherine out of it? It wasn't her fault. Any of it. She'd just walked into it because she wanted to be with him. What was waiting for them out there?

He crossed the room to the bed and stood over her. He wasn't sure how best to wake her. If it happened too quickly, she'd end up with a headache. And that was the last thing she wanted if they were travelling. He pulled the duvet back and put his hand on her shoulder. He stroked the smooth skin, slowly and gently.

She stirred and her head turned towards him. He brushed the hair from her face. She opened her eyes, then rubbed them with her thumb and forefinger, groaning as she did so.

"Oh God. I'm so sorry. I'm really so sorry".

"Who are you apologising to? Me or God?" he said with a smile.

She lifted herself up on her elbows. Then she screwed her eyes up and blinked, focussing on things around her.

"How do you feel?" he said, passing his hand across her forehead.

"Not as bad as I deserve to. Throwing it all up probably helped".

"Quite likely. Now what do think about getting up?"

"I reckon I could make it. Just get me loads of coffee. Seriously Gavin, I'm really sorry for last night. I just hope I didn't look too much of a pratt. It was supposed to be our romantic evening out in Paris".

"No problem. We're together, that's the main thing. And we've started to sort things out. For us I mean. It feels to me like we've got a future. Even if we can't fill in all the details. And I know I want to be with you".

He lifted her face to his and kissed her full on the lips.

"I love you" she said. "Now get me that coffee or I'll feel like crap all day long".

She swung her legs over the edge of the bed and sat for a moment with her head in her hands. Then she stood up, went into the bathroom and closed the door. He heard the noise of the shower.

. . .

By ten o'clock, they had checked out of the hotel and were on their way to the Gare du Nord. The weather was holding and once again the sky over Paris was clear and blue. After her shower and three cups of the strong black coffee Gavin Salter had ordered, Catherine was fully recovered and they walked briskly along the street, holding hands, making trivial conversation and savouring the morning.

They stopped at a café to buy baguettes and pastries to eat on the train. Salter was working hard not to let Catherine see how nervous he still was after the events of the previous day. But his hesitant manner and frequent glances over his shoulder told her what she had guessed anyway, and she occasionally squeezed his hand and smiled reassuringly. He felt relieved and happy that she was there.

At the station they bought tickets for the twelve thirteen scheduled to get into London by one-thirty. Then shortly before departure, they bought coffee and mineral water and boarded the train.

The tall, blonde haired man in the light-grey suit with a copy of Paris Match folded under his arm had been watching them since they arrived at the station. As they boarded, he pressed a button on his mobile.

"They're on their way. About thirteen thirty, your time". He spoke in English with a French accent.

. . .

Gavin Salter stared absent-mindedly out of the window as the French countryside rolled by. Catherine had drifted into sleep, her head on one side. The table top in front of them was littered with crumbs from the baguettes and pastries they'd eaten. The coffee cups were now empty.

He thought about Hadleigh Bridge and everything that went with it. Sunday mornings with their tea and sociable chatter at the back of the church after the service. The church committees and their endless deliberations. The constant demands on his time. The sermons he laboured over. The things he loved and the things that infuriated him. It all seemed a million miles away.

He decided he'd go to the police as soon as he got back. He'd have to spend a bit of time sorting out what he'd say to them.

However he put it, it would sound absurd and they'd be bound to wonder if he was making it up for some strange reason. In fact, as Paris and Vienna receded into the distance behind him, it all felt less and less real.

Catherine woke up and blinked.

"Where are we?"

"Coming up to the tunnel".

"I could use some more coffee".

"Do you want me to get some?"

She slipped her hand into his. "No, don't bother. Let's just stay here. Being with you on a train is great. It's really soothing".

He leaned over and kissed her forehead. "That's fine with me. I never thought a seat on a railway carriage could feel so good".

For a moment they sat in silence.

"So what are you going to tell them?" said Catherine.

"Who?"

"The police".

"How did you know I was thinking that?"

"Because it's what I was thinking. I can't make sense of it any more than you can, but they sound like a pretty mean crowd and dangerous too. It's obviously an international operation of some kind and they could be into people trafficking or any number of other things. Maybe you found the tip of the iceberg. They obviously wanted to use you for something, or why did they go to such lengths to fool you? Someone needs to be told about it all, however crazy it sounds".

"You're right. Someone needs to be told"

"So what proof have you got to show them?"

"Nothing really. No hard evidence. There was the hotel booking in Bratislava that Anderek made. But that trail has probably gone cold by now".

"How about the emails they sent you? And this institute's website. Surely they could use that to track Anderek down".

"Maybe. But you can bet the website's been closed down by now. The emails must have come from somewhere and the addresses looked genuine enough. But that doesn't mean the same person's still sitting on the other end. And in any case, an expert can always hack into a system".

They sat in silence again, still holding hands.

"So, you just tell the police what you know and what you saw happen" said Catherine. "That's all you can do. They'll just have to take it from there".

Suddenly they were in the Channel Tunnel. Catherine fell asleep again.

Chapter 24

Gavin Salter had never been much of a patriot. But as he listened to the wheels of his suitcase clicking on the platform at St Pancras as they walked towards the escalator, he thought what a good feeling it was to be back in England. He realised now how scared he had been on occasions in the last few days. He sensed he wasn't quite out of the wood yet. But he felt he had a measure of control over what happened next. It wouldn't be long now before he'd be able to contact the police and tell them his story. They'd find it hard to believe, but then so did he when he looked at it objectively. At least they'd have to take him seriously. This would be one time when being a priest would come in handy.

They walked through the automatic doors and into the busy station hall, stopping for a moment to look around at the shops and cafés and get their bearings. After sleeping for most of the journey, Catherine had woken up as the train pulled in. They'd agreed that getting a large mug of tea was the priority, because they'd both missed it so much in France. Then they'd figure out whether it was best to go to a police station somewhere in London or travel on to Hadleigh Bridge. They knew the local police through their work and they were on friendly terms with the senior officers. But although neither of them said it, they were both thinking the same thing. That someone could be here in London waiting for them. That their lives could be at risk at that very moment. And that the sooner they put the whole thing in the hands of the authorities, the sooner they would be safe.

Catherine squeezed his hand and grinned at him. "The taxis are that way" she said, pointing to one of the signs overhead. "Why don't we treat ourselves to one? I know it'll cost a bit to Waterloo, but I really can't face the tube. What do you reckon?"

"I'll go for that" said Salter. "We deserve it". And they held hands and walked in the direction the arrow was pointing.

"Do you know, I'm actually hungry again" said Catherine. "I can't believe it after all that eating we've been doing. Heaven knows what my waistline is going to look like".

"You're waistline is gorgeous, just like it's always been. Anyway, I'm hungry too. We've been using a lot of energy. We could stop off at one of these places and grab something quick. A bacon sandwich kind of interests me. And that mug of tea, of course. How does that sound to you?"

"It sounds just great" said Catherine, and slipping both arms round his waist, she hugged him as they walked.

"Careful, you're in England now" said Salter. "And that copper's giving us a funny look".

"What copper? I can't see one"

"The one over there. Just by the escalator" Catherine's eyes followed his pointing finger.

"Maybe he's feeling lonely and wants to do it too". She giggled and hugged him again.

The uniformed police officer was only a few yards ahead of them now. Suddenly Salter realised he was walking towards them, as if he meant to cut them off.

He drew level with them.

"Excuse me, sir. May I speak to you a moment?"

"By all means, officer" said Salter, gently disengaging himself from Catherine's arms and standing the suitcase upright.

The police officer looked hard at their faces, slowly moving his gaze from one to the other. Salter felt uneasy. Catherine had taken hold of his hand.

"May I see your passports?"

Salter reached into the inside pocket of his leather coat and took out his passport. Catherine had produced hers from the small haversack.

The police officer took the passports and opened them. Again he looked hard at their faces, this time for several seconds. Catherine's grip tightened.

"I must ask you to come with us".

The word 'us' made them both look to their left. Two men had appeared as if from nowhere. Another uniformed officer and a man in a light-coloured trench coat.

Salter started saying "What the hell ... "

"Don't worry" said Catherine in a whisper. "It's got to be a mistake of some kind. We haven't done anything!"

"Do as you're asked and there won't be any trouble" said the first uniformed officer. "Now just follow me".

He turned and started walking, the other two men following closely behind. At first, they continued in the direction of the taxis. Then he led them off to the right, past a ticket office, then to the left past shops and a restaurant. They turned into a steel-lined corridor, and suddenly they seemed to have left the station with its noise and bustle behind them. The first uniformed man stopped in front of a door. He pushed it open, gesturing for them to go in.

The room they now found themselves in had no windows. It was painted grey and the walls were bare. At the far end of the room was another door. Strip lighting blazed from the ceiling. A few tubular metal chairs stood around and in the centre was a large table. The man in the trench coat closed the door behind them and clicked the latch.

"Can you please tell us what this is about" said Catherine, the tension showing in her voice. None of them answered. Then the second uniformed officer lifted Salter's case onto the table.

"Your haversack" he said, looking at Catherine. She slipped it off her shoulders and handed it to him.

The man in the trench coat now spoke. "Sit down over there". He indicated two of the chairs. As they sat down, all three of the men moved to the opposite side of the table so that they faced them.

One of the uniformed men unzipped the case. Then pausing briefly, he turned the case round. He lifted the lid and held it open. Salter realised that the lid was obscuring his view and that he couldn't see what they were doing behind it.

The man in the trench coat reached into the case and appeared to be moving his hand through the contents. Then abruptly his hand stopped moving. He looked at each of the two uniformed men in turn. Then the one who was holding the lid of the case open let it drop. The man in the trench coat was holding a small polythene bag filled with a white powder.

He stared at Salter and Salter felt his throat tighten.

The man continued to stare, his gaze unblinking, as he passed the polythene bag to one of the uniformed officers. The officer examined it closely then took a small penknife out of his pocket. He opened the blade and cut what appeared to be adhesive tape around the neck of the bag. He passed it back to the man in the trench coat, who put his thumb and forefinger into the bag and took a pinch of the white powder. He held it first to his nose, then put it on the tip of his tongue. Then he brushed the remains of the powder off his fingers.

"I suppose you understand the seriousness of possessing heroin and attempting to bring it into this country. You will now both be taken to a police station and charged with possession of illegal drugs". He spoke the words slowly, his voice low and menacing.

Gavin Salter jumped to his feet with such force the chair fell to the floor behind him.

"What on earth is going on here? You know damn well that wasn't anywhere in my luggage! You planted it there yourself! This is nothing but a set-up! What is it you're trying to do for God's sake? What the hell is this about?"

"You're not helping yourself" said the man in the trench coat. "If you try and resist arrest, you'll be in it even deeper".

Salter felt as if he was losing his grip on reality. He clenched his fists and took a deep breath to calm himself. Then he turned to Catherine.

"Look, you must have seen them plant that stuff!"

"I didn't see anything" said Catherine. And looking into her face, he realised with horror that there was doubt in her eyes.

"This way" said the man in the trench coat, pointing in the direction of the other door.

Again the first uniformed man led the way, the second gesturing for them to follow. As Catherine stood up, Salter reached out to take her hand, but without looking at him she walked ahead.

They walked through another room and turned into a narrow corridor. A few yards on, the first uniformed man opened a door.

They stepped through the door into the open air. Salter felt a breeze on his face and he was grateful for its refreshing effect. But before he had a chance to look around and work out where he was, the first uniformed man opened the rear doors of a large black van that was parked ahead of them.

"Get inside" came the command from the man in the trench coat. Salter realised that whatever this was all about, this man was the one in charge.

The inside of the van was lit by a powerful light, so that everything could be seen in sharp detail. Bench seats, each with space for two to three people, were fitted against the sides. There was a ventilation grill near the roof and through it daylight could be seen, but there were no windows. Oddly, the floor was carpeted.

Salter got in first, Catherine following. She didn't look at him as they sat down beside each other. The second of the two uniformed men got in and sat opposite them. The doors slammed with a dull metallic sound and a voice crackled through an unseen intercom.

"Alright?"

"Ready" replied the uniformed man. The van pulled slowly away.

The man looked at them. "The door's locked electronically,

so don't think you can get out" he said in a flat tone.

Salter closed his eyes. For a brief moment he wondered if he should pray. Then Catherine spoke.

"At least tell us where we're going!"

The uniformed man sat perfectly still and looked at the floor. He didn't reply.

Salter tried to work out the direction in which they were heading, but they had already made several turns and he realised he'd lost track. He looked at the ventilation grill. The light through it flickered as they passed buildings but he could get no sense of where they were.

He looked at Catherine. Her brow was creased and she seemed to be deep in thought.

"I really have no idea what all this is about or how that stuff got there" he said. She didn't answer.

"I know how it looks, but you have to believe me. I'm telling the truth".

"Just like you told the truth before?" she said without turning her head.

Salter felt utterly defeated. He knew there was nothing he could say to her now. All he could do was wait for the next thing to happen in this nightmare.

They drove on at speeds of twenty to twenty-five, turning frequently. Occasionally they stopped for what must have been red lights. He could hear the noise of busy London traffic. After what seemed ages, he looked at his watch and figured they'd been going for nearly an hour.

The van slowed down and stopped. Suddenly they could no longer hear traffic noise. The van's engine was turned off and there was an eerie silence.

Catherine turned and looked at him. "Here's where we find out what kind of mess you've got us into" she said icily.

The doors of the van swung open and the other two men stood there.

"Get out" said the man in the trench coat.

They stepped out onto the concrete floor of a covered area. Salter made a quick attempt to look around and make sense of where they were. He noted high doors with bolts and heavy-duty locks which he guessed the van had just driven through, and wires and cables running along the walls. Then the man in the trench coat spoke again.

"This way".

He opened a door close to where the vehicle had stopped and led the way through into a narrow corridor. They had walked for only a few yards when he stopped and opened another door.

The room they were in was small and was clearly an office. Desks with telephones and computers were pushed against the walls, and a woman in police uniform sat at one of the desks. She stood up as they came in.

"Here they are" said the man in the trench coat.

The woman nodded. She stared at Salter.

"Empty your pockets".

One of the uniformed men held out a plastic tray. Salter removed his watch, then took his wallet and a bunch of keys out of his pockets. He placed the items in the tray. Catherine did the same with her watch, keys and a few coins

The woman opened a drawer in one of the desks and removed two objects which Salter recognised immediately as hand-held metal detectors. She passed one to the other uniformed man.

"Lift your arms above your heads and stand with your legs apart".

Walking across the room to where Catherine was standing, she ran the metal detector over Catherine's arms and legs and up and down her body. The uniformed man followed the same procedure with Salter. Then he looked at the woman and they nodded to each other. Just like mechanical figures, thought Salter.

Without another word, the woman replaced the metal detectors in the draw and sat down again. The uniformed man held the tray out to them and they retrieved their possessions. Then the man in the trench coat opened the door through which they had entered and once more led the way along the corridor.

Salter felt himself edging towards the state of mind he had always feared most. A sense of despair and powerlessness. He'd never imagined himself falling into the hands of corrupt police officers. Now that he had, he could see no way out of it. Who was there to speak on his behalf when those three were obviously all in it together and Catherine didn't believe him? What were they up to? Had they really mistaken him for someone else? Like a known drug smuggler? Had they planted the stuff just to nail a criminal they'd been chasing for some time? Or had they just picked on a complete stranger to show their superiors they were on the ball in this so-called war-on-drugs? Was he just being made convenient use of by some bent coppers hoping to climb the promotion ladder?

Then another thought came to him. Maybe these guys hadn't planted it at all. Maybe it had been there in his suitcase all the time. How did he know those goons who'd been chasing him hadn't put it there? One of them could have been on the train. He hadn't locked the case when he'd put it on the luggage rack. He hadn't thought it was worth it, he and Catherine were sitting only a couple of feet away. It would have taken seconds to unzip the case far enough to slip the polythene bag in. And passengers were walking up and down the carriages all the time, so finding cover would have been an easy matter.

Either way he had no defence. And this had really messed things up with Catherine. Now there'd be no way of putting it all back together. She'd probably go down with him as an accomplice. And she'd never forgive him for that. Not for the rest of his life.

The man in the trench coat stopped and turned round. They were standing by a lift. He pressed the call button. Somewhere on another floor the lift whirred into action and began its slow descent. It clunked to a halt and the doors slid open.

The lift was large and spacious. They stepped in, surrounded by reflections of themselves in mirrors. The man in the trench coat pressed the button for the fifth floor and the lift glided upwards. It stopped and they got out.

Nothing had prepared Salter for what he saw. They were now in a completely different place. The floor of the corridor that stretched ahead of them was covered in a thick fitted carpet and tastefully framed pictures hung at intervals on the wall. The conditioned air was cool and there was a slight scent of fresh paint. The man in the trench coat walked ahead.

Salter looked out of the corner of his eye at Catherine. She was looking around, clearly as surprised as he was.

Then he suddenly realised the uniformed men had disappeared.

The man in the trench coat turned a corner at the end of the corridor and opened the door that was now facing them.

"Father Salter and Miss Laurence. I'm so pleased you have finally arrived. Do come in".

Chapter 25

THE MAN SEATED ON THE leather chair behind the wide desk was black and probably in his middle forties. He wore gold-rimmed glasses and was dressed in a dark blue suit. He had the confident air of one in a position of authority and the clear, resonant voice had an unmistakeable Caribbean lilt.

"Please sit down. I'm sure you need to after your journey" he said with a broad smile, spreading his hands to indicate the two armchairs in front of the desk.

"Who are you?" said Salter "And where are we?"

"My name is Benjamin James" he said, rising to his feet. "And I am ... well ... there's no point trying to explain to you who I am. My work is subject to the Official Secrets Act and I'm not allowed to talk about it to anyone. Even my family don't really know what I do". He gave the broad smile again.

"Then at least tell us what the hell's going on, because now I've completely lost the plot. For a start, this place doesn't look like any police station I've ever been in. I thought I was going to be charged with trafficking drugs".

"Father Salter" said James "I will gladly explain things to you. But first, I need to ask you one very important question".

He paused.

"Would you like tea or coffee?"

Salter turned to look at Catherine. She was already staring at him, wide-eyed with her mouth slightly open.

"Er .. I suppose ... tea ... please" he stammered. Catherine nodded.

"That's fine" said James, and he walked across the room to a small trolley on which two large vacuum jugs stood, together with a collection of white cups and saucers.

"Sugar?" he said, looking sideways at them. They shook their heads.

He pressed the lever on one of the jugs and tea flowed into the cup he was holding.

"As I said, please make yourselves comfortable". He waited for them to sit down before walking back across the room and handing them two cups of tea. They both took a mouthful. It was hot and full-flavoured and it felt good. James sat behind the desk and leaned back in the leather chair.

"Now" he said, taking a deep breath and placing the tips of his fingers together. "You've probably guessed that this is not a police station and I'm not a police officer".

"Yes, we had at least figured that out" said Catherine.

"Okay" said James. "Now where's the best place to start?" And he clasped his hands and stared down at the surface of the desk, his brow slightly creased.

"Maybe I should begin by telling you where you are".

He stood up and walked over to the middle of the room's three windows. All three were hung with Venetian blinds and the slats were closed. He pressed a button and the slats opened with an electric buzzing sound.

Salter rose to his feet and crossed the room to where James

was standing. He peered through the window at the skyline that was now visible.

James pointed with his finger. "That large building over there. You can just see it through the trees. Can you tell me what it is?"

Salter took a step closer to the window.

"Well, it looks a bit like ... hang on a minute ... that's the Tate Gallery!"

James burst into jovial laughter. "Well done, Father Salter! You know your London alright! By the way, that stretch of water down there is called the Thames, in case you were wondering".

Salter turned to look at him, an expression of blank disbelief on his face.

"So that means we're ... "

"In the headquarters of MI6".

Catherine had got up from her chair and was now standing with them.

"But that's impossible!" she said, her eyes wide and staring. "We must have been driving for an hour. And you're telling us we're only a mile or two from where we got off the train!"

"Your journey was not what it seemed" said James. "The driver had been instructed to take a roundabout trip through every side street she could find. It was necessary to do so".

"What do you mean, necessary?" Salter snapped the reply.

"For your protection. In case the vehicle was being followed. We couldn't risk them knowing where you were being taken".

"This isn't making any sense" said Catherine. "A minute ago I thought we were being taken to a police station and done for drug smuggling. Now you're telling us we're in MI6 headquarters".

"Who did you think might be following the vehicle?" said Salter.

Then he paused as realisation began to seep slowly into his mind.

"Is this something to do with ... ?"

"Why don't we sit down again?" said James, and his voice had the calm and comforting tone of a counsellor. The three of them returned to their chairs.

"Can I first of all apologise to you both for the way in which you were brought here. We needed to get you here with the minimum of fuss and we figured if you thought you were being arrested you'd be more likely to comply".

"So the heroin was a plant" said Salter.

James nodded. "The officer in the coat had it in his pocket. It was a crude trick, but we didn't have time for anything more sophisticated".

"We haven't committed any crimes then" said Catherine.

James smiled and shook his head. "At least not any that I know about".

"Gavin, I'm really sorry" said Catherine. And she reached across and took hold of his hand.

"That's the easy bit over with" said James, leaning back in his chair and folding his hands in his lap. "The rest of it's a bit more complicated". He looked at Salter.

"Father Salter. You may not yet be in possession of all the details, but I think you have already begun to work out that you have been the victim of an elaborate hoax. And my guess is that it was all going very smoothly until something happened to make you suspicious. That was when you left Bratislava in an obvious hurry".

Salter nodded. "So are you telling me I was being watched by MI6?"

"From the moment you left London. But what was it that went wrong? What exactly raised your suspicions and when did it happen?"

"It was the day in Presov and a conversation over lunch. Somebody calling himself Janovic and claiming to be an expert on the New Testament came out with something that was utter nonsense. I spotted it immediately. If he'd been a genuine scholar, he'd never have said any such thing. He'd have known it was completely wrong".

"Can you describe the man?"

Salter paused to recollect. "I reckon he was fifty or so. I remember he had very thick eyebrows. His hair was thick too, and it was grey. He was quite muscular. And his face was lined, especially round the eyes".

"And his clothes?"

"I think he had a grey suit on. Nothing fancy".

James leaned forward and put his elbows on the desk. He nodded, slowly and thoughtfully.

"That just about fits the description of a body that was found on some waste ground outside Presov in the early hours of Thursday. Throat cut. Sounds like they got rid of him when they realised he'd given everything away".

He leaned back in the chair again.

"So what was their story line? How did they persuade you to go out to Slovakia?"

"They told me there was something very ancient buried in my churchyard. Something to do with a visit to Britain by St Paul. The trip out to Slovakia was all about seeing the evidence for myself".

"And once they'd succeeded in convincing you, what were you supposed to do about it?"

"Well, the man who came to see me, his name was Anderek ..."

"So that's what he's calling himself these days!" Once again James burst into his jovial laugh. "No wonder we have such trouble keeping up with him! But I'm sorry, Father Salter, I interrupted you. Please continue".

"He told me all I had to do was let a team of researchers use the churchyard for a few days and plug their laptops into a socket in the church hall. Then if they found what they were looking for, I could take the credit for it. Maybe even get a job with this institute he worked for".

James stroked his chin.

"They weren't interested in your churchyard, I can tell you that. Except as a convenient place to give them cover. Until they'd done what they'd really come there to do".

"And what was that?" said Catherine.

"They were going to blow up the London Underground. And they were planning to do it on a far bigger scale than what happened in 2005. And with a much higher level of destruction and fatality".

"God" said Salter under his breath. James paused to let what he had said sink in. Then he continued.

"This wouldn't have been three or four suicide bombers with exploding haversacks killing a few people who happened to be sitting near them. The idea was to plant small amounts of very powerful material over a wide area of the network. Each one would have been carefully concealed and linked to an electronic trigger in a pyramid structure, so that one trigger would set off several explosions. These would have been activated by a central command at exactly the same time, thus maximising the demoralising effect on the population of London. And the damage done ... "

James breathed in deeply, then sighed.

"It's better not even to think about it. I could roughly describe the state of London's infrastructure after such an event and tell you what contingency plans the security services would put into operation. But that would just be words and figures. The death and suffering that would have resulted are beyond imagining".

For a moment they all sat in silence. Then Salter spoke.

"And I was very nearly an accomplice in all that".

James looked at him and raised his eyebrows. "Now don't start blaming yourself, for God's sake! You were caught up in a very carefully crafted deception. I bet this Anderek guy gave you website addresses and business cards and heaven knows what else. All to make you think it was on the level".

"Yes, that's exactly what he did. I emailed one of his colleagues and got a reply back. And I visited their supposed website. The Institute for Historical and Cultural Research, based in Bratislava. Part of the Ministry of Education and Science, according to him. He told me it was a joint initiative with the Ministry of Culture".

James smiled and nodded.

"You've got to admire these people. They're real professionals. Basically what they did was to lay a trail that looked impressive but actually led nowhere. They invented a totally fictitious organisation with its own website which would have fooled you straight away because I'm guessing you don't speak the language. As for the email you received, they probably had one of their own people working on the inside, maybe in a government office. Or they'd managed to break into the system somehow. And if you'd taken your investigation further, say by contacting the ministry direct, they'd probably have passed your phone call from one department to the other because they didn't know what you were talking about. We all know what government departments are like. Eventually you'd have given up. And if you'd actually managed to speak to someone and they'd told you they'd never heard of this institute, well this Anderek person would probably have had an answer for that as well. If a ministry has a large number of sections, is it surprising if they don't all know about each other? Or he could have said you'd just happened to speak to someone who was new in the job. You can explain anything if you're clever enough. And these people are".

"So who exactly are they?" said Catherine. "And what do you know about them? They're obviously a criminal gang of some kind".

"We know a bit about them, Miss Laurence. But I can assure you that to call them a criminal gang is seriously to underestimate their capability. If that's all they were, we'd have rounded them up by now without too much difficulty. The fact is we're dealing here with an international organisation with some very powerful connections".

He paused. Once again he was letting his words sink in.

"The nerve centre of their operations is a private security outfit based in Geneva. You will understand if I don't tell you their name. Now on the surface it's a quite legitimate business. The Americans have used them in Iraq and they've had contracts with the United Nations to provide security for aid projects. And, as I said, they have good connections. Their bosses hang out with Swiss politicians all the time and you often see them in Berlin, Paris, London or wherever. But they're also a front for some pretty nasty stuff. In the last few years they've been dealing drugs big time. They've acted as brokers for all kinds of arms shipments. They're known to have handled cluster bombs and landmines and they don't care who they sell to as long as they make a big profit. And this is where your Anderek fits in".

"So that's not his real name" said Salter.

"No it's not. His real name is Jurinko Valach and he's a particularly unpleasant piece of work. Now we don't actually know what he looks like. The word is he's quite stylish. Into expensive clothes and that sort of thing. But we have no recent photographs of him and the ones we have aren't much use because he often uses disguise and he's even been known to change his facial appearance. That makes tracking him very difficult. But we do know that he's Slovakian by birth and that he was briefly in the army as part of a commando unit towards the end of the Communist era. He joined the security firm as a regular mercenary, but they soon noticed how ruthless he was, not to mention his propensity for violence and his skill in the use of torture. So he was redeployed, as you might say. And he was an obvious choice to head up this operation for them".

"I'm with you so far" said Catherine. "But something's not making sense. Hadleigh Bridge is over thirty miles from London. If they were planning to blow up the London Underground, why didn't they get a bit closer?"

"Too dangerous. They had some pretty sophisticated equipment to put together and it was going to take time. And they needed to test it thoroughly before they used it for the real thing. Security's tight in London. We've got undercover agents working everywhere and the centre's under constant surveillance. They couldn't run the risk of raising suspicion or being discovered. In a place like Hadleigh Bridge, they could work undisturbed for as long as they needed to. Particularly if they'd got the local priest to cover for them. Then they'd move their stuff to London when they were ready. And of course they would cover their tracks. Which would undoubtedly have involved killing you, Father Salter, because by then you would have known too much".

"So how did your people find out about all this?" said Salter.

"The German police in Frankfurt picked up one of their guys for a motoring offence. At first they didn't realise who they'd got. Then they ran a routine check and found he was on Interpol's books. So they offered him a deal. Freedom from prosecution, a brand new identity and a one-way ticket to Latin America in exchange for information. And he talked. He was only small-fry but he knew all about the London business. He was the one that told us Valach was involved. And he pinpointed Hadleigh Bridge and St Mary's Church. That's when we homed in on you".

"Right" said Catherine. "But this still isn't fitting together. If what they're about is making cash out of drugs and armaments, why would they want to wreck the London tube network? That's the kind of thing you'd expect a terrorist group to do. What good would it do them?"

James folded his arms and looked across the room to the windows. The expression on his face was one of genuine perplexity.

"This is where it all gets rather murky. I said this security firm has its headquarters in Geneva. But it also has links to America. It's owned and financed by a very odd character that we've had our eye on for a long time. He's a billionaire and he lives in Texas most of the time, although he has homes in New York, Boston and one or two other places. No-one knows quite how much money he's got, but he's generally reckoned to be one of the ten wealthiest people in the world. Again I can't tell you his name and I'm not sure you'd have heard of him anyway. He's very reclusive. If he travels, it's with his own fleet of private jets or a custom-made limousine the size of a house".

Salter sat forward in the chair. "So why would an American billionaire want to mount an attack on London? What motive could he possibly have?"

"I couldn't say for certain. But we do know enough about him to give us at least some insight into what his motivation might be and why he should want to inflict destruction on such a scale. As I said a moment ago, the whole thing's very murky. You see, he's one of these fundamentalist Christians. You'd know all about them and I'm sure I don't have to tell you how odd some of them are. He belongs to a church that only operates in the Southern States. It's pretty small as churches go, especially in America. Just a few hundred members. And like everything else he's associated with, he practically owns it. It certainly runs largely on his money. Now these church people are a very secretive lot. We're not even sure what they call themselves. You have to be recommended and vetted before you can take part in their services and there's a long wait after that before you can join them as a full member. Effectively it's a secret society. Because of our interest in him, we've been trying to infiltrate them for years, and just recently, by working with the CIA, we managed to get an agent in there. Now he's been sending us some very interesting and very disturbing reports. Like many fundamentalists, they have this thing about the end of the world being immanent. But they have a somewhat different approach. You see, they don't just sit around on mountain tops because they think it's going to happen any moment.

They seem to have this idea that they could actually help to bring it about".

"What?" Salter was now on the edge of his seat.

"According to them, what goes on in certain countries is particularly abhorrent to God. This is what our agent's been picking up in conversations he's heard and things he's read. For example, they reckon France is drifting into communism because of the strength of its trade unions. But the place they've really got it in for is Britain, and for a whole host of reasons. Our attitudes to homosexuality are too liberal. We have too many Muslims here. Too many young girls are getting pregnant. You get the idea. Now sinners have to be punished and, as they see it, it's their job to administer the punishment in no uncertain fashion. And when God sees this happening, then he'll decide it's time for the Second Coming and Jesus will float down to earth on a cloud and send everyone to hell for eternity, except of course the handful of people who belong to this peculiar church of theirs".

He paused, then leaned across the desk and looked at Salter.

"I hope you don't think I'm ridiculing religion, Father Salter".

Salter was resting his forehead on his hands. He shook his head.

"No, no. I don't think that at all. My God, this really is frightening".

"Indeed it is" said James. "So this plot to blow up the London Underground probably started life in the mind of this religious lunatic and his friends in Texas as a form of retribution against Britain. It's certainly ironic that they wanted to drag you and your church into it. Maybe that had some significance for them. Maybe it was symbolic in their twisted scheme of things".

"But why can't you do something about this weirdo?" said Catherine. "Surely at the very least he's guilty of conspiracy to murder!"

James spread his hands wide in a gesture of exasperation.

"We've no proof. At least nothing that would stand up against him. We can't even prove the link between him and the security firm. It operates through a whole network of completely independent companies. And he's a powerful man with some very powerful friends. Over the years he's bought himself influence. And he's surrounded by an army of lawyers. Any legal action against him would be quietly dropped before it got anywhere near a court and whoever instigated it would lose their job the next day. All we can hope to do is keep tabs on this outfit and get as much information as we can on their operations so that we can at least fight them on the ground".

Catherine sat back in the chair, folded her arms and sighed.

"Alright. I can see what you're up against".

"Thank you Miss Laurence. I'm grateful to you for understanding".

"You say you've been watching me since I left London" said Salter.

"If not us, then our counterparts in Europe. We've been working closely together on this one".

"Can you throw any light on some of the strange things that were happening?"

"Yes, I think I can. For a start, you were right to get away from Bratislava when you did. Valach, or Anderek as you knew him, must have realised your suspicions had been raised. If you'd confronted him, he'd have killed you there and then. He had no reason to bother with formalities. And by the time you got to Vienna, he'd got someone on your tail".

"The man in the blue sweatshirt? The one who ended up dead in the street?"

"That was him. We had difficulty spotting him at first. He was pretty good. He knew how to keep low. But we saw him just in time. Soon after you left the Landtmann. He got ahead of you on the metro and when you got off at Südtiroler Platz, he was waiting for you. He'd managed to get into one of the buildings and he'd positioned himself on a stairwell by a window. He had a really fancy sniper's rifle in that bag he was carrying. The Austrian police seized the bag when they arrived at the scene and they're examining the rifle closely. They think it was made in Russia. Small parts, easily concealed, but quick assembly. And it packed a real punch. You wouldn't have stood a chance. Our man tried to disarm him but ending up having to shoot him. The guy ran for it but he couldn't get far with the wound he'd got. He died in the street. That was when you saw him".

"And the hit-and-run in Paris?"

"Well of course that was them again. And this time they nearly succeeded, as I think you're probably aware. We had a tail on you from the moment you got off at the Gare de l'Est and we were watching you as you went to cross that street, but we didn't realise what the white car was doing until it was nearly on top of you. Good thing you reacted quickly. We put out an alert but the car was dumped just a few minutes later. It'd been stolen of course. The driver just disappeared".

"I'm surprised they didn't have another go at me after that".

"They did. At least they were going to. They had one of their nastiest killers waiting for you yesterday at the Gare du Nord and he was all kitted out to do the poison needle trick. You'd have felt a scratch on your ankle, then it would've been two or three minutes at the most before you were heading for the pearly gates. We tipped off the French police and they picked him up. My guess is he'll co-operate and tell them a bit about the organisation. If he doesn't, he'll go down for a very long time and I doubt if he'll want to be a martyr for the cause".

"And what about today? I wasn't aware of any strange goings-on".

"We carried on watching you in Paris and one of our agents got on Eurostar with you. We figured when the guy with the needle was nicked they'd try something else, either on the train or at the other end. If they were waiting for you at St Pancras, they would have been scared off when they saw you arrested. Even so we didn't take any risks when we drove you here. Now the word will get back to them soon and they'll know that we know, so the London operation will have to be called off. Obviously we'll be keeping a careful eye on things, but they won't be able to do what they'd planned to do. And we'll have made a very large dent in their armour".

"So what now?" said Catherine. "Is there any chance we'll ever have a normal life again? They know who we are and where we live. Won't they want to get their own back one day? From what you've said, they're not the sort of people who'd forgive and forget. Or were you planning to give us new passports and new identities and pack us off to South America?"

James took the gold-rimmed glasses off and rubbed his eyes. Then he put the glasses back on and folded his arms on the desk.

"I hear what you're saying, Miss Laurence. And of course I couldn't rule out the possibility of reprisals and I'd be lying if I tried to. But really I don't think you need to go and hide on the other side of the world somewhere. We can give you discrete police protection for a while and we'll probably do that. But remember, this organisation has had a real bloody nose as a result of all this. They won't want to go hanging about in the UK for a good many years. Valach will certainly be keeping out of our way for a long time yet. And in that line of business, life expectancy isn't great. He'll be dead before long. If the law doesn't get him then one of his enemies will. And grudges tend to be a personal thing. Once they've got new operations going with new people running them, they won't be interested in you".

Catherine bit her lower lip. "Let's hope you're right".

"All this stuff you've been telling us" said Salter. "Isn't it, well, confidential at least?"

James nodded.

"We certainly weren't planning to put it in the News of

the World. And we'd like an undertaking from you that what you've heard today you'll keep to yourselves. But then even if you did start telling your friends all about it, who the hell's going to believe you? I mean, it sounds just like the plot of a spy thriller, doesn't it?"

And he gave the broad smile.

They sat in silence for a few moments. Then James reached into the inside pocket of his jacket and took out a tan pigskin wallet. He opened it and took out two small white cards, then placed them on the desk in front of him. Each card had a single line of figures printed on it.

"Father Salter. Miss Laurence. I am now going to ask you to leave this office accompanied by a member of my staff. They will take you to another room in this building where some of our officers will question you in more detail about your recent experiences. I'm sure you will both be most helpful to them, as you have been to me. In the unlikely event that you need to contact us in future, please use the telephone number printed on the card. Meanwhile, I would recommend that you rest from your ordeal by spending two or three nights in a good hotel here in London and eating out at a few good restaurants".

"It's very kind of you to suggest that, but it could work out a bit expensive for us. So if it's all the same to you, we'll just go quietly home" said Salter.

James looked at him. "If you would like to check the balance of your bank account, you will find the sum of five thousand pounds has been deposited".

Salter's jaw dropped open.

"Please don't misunderstand me" said James "but I hope I never see either of you again".

Chapter 26

"Would you like to try some, madam?"

The young woman in the trouser suit and high heels smiled her regulation lipstick-coated smile and the heavily powdered cheeks dimpled as they were obviously meant to. Catherine Laurence pulled the sleeve of her shirt up and the young woman dabbed the exposed wrist with the glass stopper. Catherine inhaled the scent luxuriously. Then she stared into the middle distance, a look of critical discernment on her face.

"Thank you, but no. It's insufficiently complex and much too heavy on the musk. And in any case, I never buy anything less expensive than Chanel Number Five". And with a swish of the calf-length cotton skirt she was wearing, she turned and walked away, leaving the young woman gazing after her and holding the glass stopper aloft in mid-air.

"God, you're such an embarrassment" said Gavin Salter frowning and looking down at the floor as he walked beside her.

"Well, it's not every day one shops in Harrod's, is it? So you might as well make the best of it. The last time I was here, a friend of mine was outside with a placard protesting about the fur trade. The two of us nearly got arrested. But they're not to know that are they?"

"What do you fancy doing next?"

"How about sex in the lift? That'd be a first for me".

"Will you shut it!" said Salter under his breath as he looked anxiously around him.

"Sorry, Father. Didn't mean to show you up". She nuzzled her face into his shoulder and kissed his neck. "Let's try the food hall. I want some of their marmalade so I can leave it in the fridge at work and impress everybody".

Salter sighed and shook his head. Then as their eyes met, they stopped and hugged each other, while shoppers and tourists swerved to avoid them and a security guard glared.

It was Monday, late morning. After two nights in a luxury hotel off Kensington High Street, a visit to one of Salter's favourite London churches and a boat trip along the Thames, they both felt relaxed and happy to be alive. The final session of questioning at MI6 had been far less arduous than they had imagined it would be and after being reunited with their luggage, they had been taken in an unmarked police car to Victoria Station where they had booked their accommodation through an agency. A phone call to one of the churchwardens at St Mary's had secured Salter an extra two days holiday on the grounds that he had just met an old friend, which under the circumstances he was able to tell them with a clear conscience. Their plan now was to spend one more night in London then travel back the following day to Hadleigh Bridge.

In the food hall, Catherine examined several jars of marmalade before making her choice. Salter joined her at the checkout.

"Save the bag" she whispered. "They're great to show off with when you go shopping".

"Let's get out of here" he said, peering at the numerous direction signs. "All this wealth's making me envious and envy's one of the deadly sins".

They pushed the heavy door and it swung open, and they stepped out into Knightsbridge.

"Do you know what I'd really like to do?" said Catherine.

"Please don't tell me".

"No seriously. I'd really like to pick up sandwiches for lunch and eat them in Green Park. I've not been there for years and it's such a lovely spot. And it would get us out of all this traffic. I'm sure these fumes aren't good for country folk like us".

"That sounds great. We'll drop into Fortnum and Mason's. Now, let's see. We can pick up the tube at Knightsbridge, it's just along the road".

"You lazy bastard! What's wrong with a good healthy walk? We could do with it after all that food and alcohol we've been putting away".

"I haven't come here to get fit. We're supposed to be enjoying ourselves. I say we get the tube".

"And I say up yours. I want to walk".

"Listen. You had your way last night with the restaurant. I wanted Greek for a change but we ended up with Italian yet again. So I get my turn today. Right?"

Catherine put on a grumpy look.

"Okay, you win this one. We'll get the tube. But I'm keeping score. Hey, stop for a moment. They've got great jewellery and stuff in here". And she pulled on his arm and guided him into a shop.

After ten minutes and a few small purchases, they left the shop and carried on towards Knightsbridge underground station.

"This is such a lovely old station" said Catherine as they descended the spiral stairs. "I hope they're not planning to modernise it or anything".

The platform was busy and when the train arrived all the seats were taken and several people were standing.

"Oh no" said Salter. "If there's one thing I hate it's being jammed into a tube carriage".

"Stop moaning. It's only two stops to Green Park. In any case, you might get jammed up against me. That'd be nice, wouldn't it?"

Salter grunted disapprovingly. The doors slid open and they got on at the front end of the carriage.

"We might as well stay here" said Catherine, leaning her head on his shoulder. "There's no room further down".

"No, I guess not. Still, like you said it's only two stops. And then it's just a short walk ... "

"Gavin! Are you alright?" She seized hold of his arm.

His face had suddenly turned pale and his eyes were wide and staring. He looked as if he were in a trance.

"What is it? What's the matter?" She held her mouth close to his ear and squeezed his arm. Suddenly he seemed to snap back to reality. He turned and looked into her face.

"Manic Yanik!"

She stared back at him. "What on earth are you talking about?"

"It's him! Yanik! He was the driver in Slovakia! He's one of them!"

"Who was? You're not making sense!"

"Down the other end! He mustn't see me!" Salter spun around and faced into the corner, his head down.

"He's the one with the short fair hair and the ring in his ear. Can you see him? For God's sake don't attract his attention!" He spoke in a low whisper.

Catherine looked towards the far end of the carriage, inclining her head to see around a man who'd moved into her field of vision.

"Yes I can see him. What did you call him?"

"Manic Yanik. He used to drive like a lunatic. Keep looking. It's Hyde Park Corner in a minute and he might get off. We mustn't lose him".

The train slowed to a halt in the tunnel, pulling away again after a few seconds. Then the recorded voice announced Hyde Park Corner and the lights of the station appeared in the windows. The doors opened. Bodies moved in and out of the carriage.

"It's alright" said Catherine. "He's still there". She leaned closer and again put her mouth against his ear.

"So what do you plan on doing?"

"We stay with him".

"But if he's one of them shouldn't we tell the police or something?"

"And how do we do that? By the time we've got off and up into the street and called them, he'll have disappeared. And God knows where he'll be then. The police might never find him. And if he's not already on their books, how will they know who to look for? I don't even know if Yanik's his real name. No, we need to follow him and find out where he's going and what he's up to".

"Is that such a good idea? After what I've heard about them, I don't fancy being a hero".

"No, nor do I. But the fact he's turned up in London doesn't make sense. Like James said, they'd have had to abandon their original plans. So what the hell's he doing here? We've got to find out".

The train drew into Green Park.

"He's still with us" said Catherine.

"I've got to stop him recognising me. He's bound to if he spots me and it'll blow everything. He'll just make a run for it and we'll lose him for good".

Catherine looked around, then reached across and picked up a newspaper from the shelf behind the seats.

"Here you are. Hang on to this".

Salter opened the paper and spread it full width, turning slowly around as he did so. Then he looked over the paper's top edge. Yanik was standing with his back to them.

"Let's just try and be relaxed about it. If we act natural, he's much less likely to notice us".

Catherine raised her eyebrows. "No problem. I trail violent criminals all the time".

They were at Piccadilly Circus. Salter half closed the paper and peered around it. Yanik didn't move as more people got on and off.

"Let's sit down" said Catherine, inclining her head to indicate two seats which had just been vacated. They sat down as the train pulled away, Salter obscuring his face from view by pretending to scratch his ear with the hand that held the paper.

"Can you still see him?" he whispered, opening the paper again.

Catherine leaned forward slightly in the seat.

"Yes I can".   "That's good. Keep watching him".

Salter flexed the muscles of his arms. They were getting stiff from the awkward way he was holding the newspaper. In his mind he ran through the things that might happen as a result of the strange pursuit he was now engaged in. He might stumble onto something too big to handle. He might end up putting his life in danger, just as he had before. And once again, he might be involving Catherine and putting her at risk along with himself.

"The next station is Leicester Square"

"Oh God, he's moving!" Catherine hissed the words as she grasped Salter's hand.

"Take it slow now. Let's get out of that door at the end so we can keep our distance".

"Right. I'll go first so you can hide behind me if he turns round".

They stepped out onto the platform. For a moment Salter was seized by panic as Yanik disappeared into the moving crowd.

"He's there" said Catherine. "I can just see the top of his head". She walked on, reaching behind to take hold of Salter's hand.

Yanik was moving slowly and several people in the crowd overtook him. For the first time Catherine noticed he was carrying a piece of luggage, the strap slung over one shoulder. From where she was, it looked to be a large holdall. A sign pointed to the Northern Line and he followed it.

When they arrived on the platform, Yanik was roughly the same distance ahead. He was facing away from them and looking into the tunnel. The holdall was at his feet.

"I dread to think what's in the bag" said Catherine.

"It could be luggage. He's come from the Heathrow direction. Maybe he's just flown in".

"Let's hope it's just luggage".

Salter knew what she was thinking. He was thinking the same.

A train roared out of the tunnel. The illuminated sign above the platform said it was bound for Edgeware. Yanik got on.

"Sit on the same side as him. I'll sit opposite you. That way I can see him but he won't see you".

Salter followed Catherine's instructions. To their relief, Yanik found a seat at the far end of the carriage. Salter stretched his legs and leaned back in his seat. He folded the newspaper and put it on his lap. For the first time in a while, he relaxed. Catherine was sitting diagonally opposite. Her hair was hanging loosely down the side of her face, so that it would have prevented Yanik seeing when she was looking in his direction. She thinks of everything, Salter thought.

The train rumbled on, going north through Euston and Camden Town. Waves of bodies got on and got off. Yanik stayed where he was, the holdall on the floor between his feet.

Once again, Salter found himself wondering with anxiety what the outcome of all this might be. Would he have the presence of mind to act if he needed to? Was he ready to meet violence with violence? He was going into the unknown. Nothing in his life so far had prepared him for the threat he might have to face in the next few hours. Or even the next few minutes. He wondered how he would protect Catherine. And then he realised that part of him was looking to her to protect him.

A sharp sound brought him back to the present moment. It was Catherine snapping her fingers to get his attention. Salter carefully leaned forward and looked around the person next to him. Yanik was standing up with the holdall slung over his shoulder.

"The next station is Hampstead"

Catherine raised her forefinger indicating for Salter to wait. The train was slowing to a halt. Yanik moved towards the door. Catherine nodded and they both stood up.

There were now only a handful of people on the train and they stepped out onto an almost empty platform. Yanik was some way ahead of them, walking slowly. Salter turned around, facing Catherine and elaborately folding the newspaper.

"Right, let's go" said Catherine and they walked in the direction of a sign that said "Way Out".

Chapter 27

"Do you know this part of London?" said Salter.
"Never been here".

"I used to know it a few years ago when I had a friend living here. I think we're sort of heading for the Heath".

"Good thing he doesn't move too fast. At least we can keep up with him without knocking ourselves out".

After coming out of Hampstead Station, Yanik had walked south for a short way before turning down a side street. He was walking purposefully, without looking around. He obviously knew exactly where he was going.

"You need a disguise of some kind in case he looks round" said Catherine. "He might just recognise you, even at this distance".

"No problem. I've got a Batman outfit in my back pocket. Carry it all the time".

"I'm serious. Have you got your shades with you?"

Salter reached into his inside pocket.

"As a matter of fact I have".

"Put 'em on. I'll give you my baseball cap. It should be in the bag".

Catherine slipped the small black haversack off her shoulders and put her hand inside.

"Here. Stick this on". She passed the cap to Salter and he put it on, pulling the brim down over the dark glasses.

"You look really stupid but it'll do for now".

"Do you think we should walk on opposite sides?"

"Probably not worth it. If we needed to communicate or move quickly it could screw things up. Best stay together".

"You're right". Salter thought how good it felt at that moment to have someone there. Suddenly being alone didn't seem as attractive as it used to.

"He's turning off. Speed up" said Catherine.

Yanik had disappeared into another side street. They quickened their pace. It crossed Salter's mind that he might have seen them following him, maybe even from the tube at Knightsbridge. That he'd recognised him and was now deliberately leading them on a false trail. Maybe into a trap. They rounded the corner and saw him again. After hurrying to catch up, they were now too close to him and they slowed down to maintain the distance. A few minutes later he turned off again and the whole procedure was repeated.

Now the surroundings were different. The road had widened out and the houses were much larger and more opulent. Yanik was walking more slowly and looking up at one particularly large house. He stopped outside and reached for the latch on the gate.

They turned to face each other and Salter took a small A-to-Z out of his pocket. He opened it and they pretended to consult it, their fingers pointing and turning the pages. The charade continued until Catherine glanced towards the house.

"Okay, he's gone in".

"Right. We get the other side of the house, so that if he's

noticed us following him it'll look as if we've just walked by".

"Isn't it time to get onto the police and tell them what we know?"

"We still don't know enough. All we've seen is him going into a big house. That's not a crime. And like I said, if he's not on their records and they've no reason to hold him, then it'll just spook him and he'll be out of here. We've got to find out something about that house. What's going on in there and why he went in".

"So what do we do? Knock on the door?"

"Yes I know it sounds mad but we've got to try at least. If we can just get a look inside somehow. Even just through a window. They could have equipment of some kind. You know what James said they were planning. We could memorise anything we see so that we can describe it in detail. Then we'll have something to say to the police. Or even to MI6. At the moment we don't have anything except one person that I've seen. And when it comes down to it, I don't know for sure who he is and where he fits into it all".

"I'm with you. Didn't want a life anyway".

"Save your sense of humour, you might need it later. Now let's just walk on like two innocent and not very bright tourists who can't find the way to where they're going".

They walked on. He passed her the book. She studied it and passed it back. They were level now with the house. With his eyes shaded by the dark glasses, Salter felt confident in looking at it obliquely. It had three storeys and a basement and the three skylights in the roof indicated a converted loft. The windows were high. Steps led up to the white-painted front door. The house had no name. Just a number. Eleven.

Catherine had been looking deliberately in the other direction. "See anything?"

"Not from here. There are net curtains at all the windows. We're going to have to get in a bit closer. Maybe we could slip down the side without being noticed and take a look at the back. There must be a garden. Maybe we could hide in it".

"You really are tired of living, aren't you?"

"We've got to do something. If they'd got away with the underground thing, right now there'd be a gaping whole in the middle of London and God knows how many dead".

"No argument there. Just don't let's take any risks".

They were past the house and out of sight of the windows. They stopped.

"Okay let's go for it" said Salter. "We'll just have to hope no-one sees us from the front. If we're challenged, we can say we were looking for the side entrance. Then we can say we made a mistake and got the wrong house. Tell them we think some old friends of ours might live at number fifteen. And just act natural".

"I've forgotten how you do that" said Catherine with a wistful look. "Anyway, what if this Yanik guy appears at the door? Won't he recognise you?"

"He might. I'll hang onto the cap and dark glasses and hope they work for a bit longer. And if the worst happens, we run for it".

Salter slipped the A-to-Z back into his pocket. Catherine walked ahead and they opened the small gate leading to a path running along the side of the house. When they came to a door, they paused, but the door was solid with no glass in it. Catherine gestured to him with crossed fingers. They carried on to the end of the path.

They turned the corner and found themselves on a concrete patio that stretched the width of the house. Its surface was cracked and badly maintained and shabby wrought iron garden furniture was scattered around. The garden was small and enclosed by a high wall. The grass on the lawn had not been cut for some time and dry and rotting leaves lay everywhere. What plants there were in the flowerbeds were dead or dying.

Up at the windows, heavy curtains were drawn. There was something strange about the place and that thought passed between them as they looked at each other.

Salter pointed to a door and they moved towards it. The glass panels had been painted thickly on the inside so that nothing could be seen through them. He put his ear against the glass. There was no sound from inside and he nodded to Catherine, then he slowly and gently turned the handle. The door opened inwards.

They were standing in a narrow passageway that stretched a few yards ahead of them before it turned off and Salter guessed it went through to the front of the house. To their left, an archway led to the foot of a small staircase.

"Now what?" whispered Catherine, putting her face close to his.

"We take a look up those stairs. They obviously go up the back of the house. We can't risk going anywhere near the front. Whoever's in the place, that's where they'll be".

"Doesn't it strike you as a bit odd to find the backdoor left unlocked?"

"It does. But there could be any reason for that. The main thing is we've got in".

"This is crazy, you know. What happens if we're discovered? Outside's a different matter. We could say we got the wrong house. But now we're inside and we're trespassing. If this guy's who you say he is, God knows what he might do to us".

"I understand what you're saying but I still think we've got a chance. This place shows all the signs of being empty. It's really weird. It's like the owner's abandoned it. Those stairs have got no carpet on. And take a look at the walls. When do you think they were last painted? The garden was a mess too. All that rusty old metal on the patio. People round here look after their houses. They spend money on them. And does it sound like anyone's around? Can you hear anything?"

Catherine shook her head.

"Right. It could be Yanik's the only one here. Maybe he's dossing here or something. If he *is* on his own, we could take him between us. If we have to, that is".

Catherine looked at him and raised her eyebrows. He could tell he wasn't convincing her.

"We've got no choice" he said. "We've got to find out something about this place. Once we've found something, then we get out quick".

He gestured towards the stairs.

The wood creaked and groaned under their feet as they moved slowly upwards, straining every nerve in their bodies in the effort not to make any noise. He suddenly noticed the smell of the place. It smelt the way a house does when no-one lives there.

At the top of the stairs, they stepped onto a landing with two doors. The walls were a grubby cream and rectangles outlined in the dirt showed where pictures had hung a long time before.

Salter put his ear to one of the doors and listened intently for several seconds. Then he opened it.

The small box-like room was completely empty. It had one small window. Yellowing wallpaper covered the walls and the floorboards were bare. The smell of emptiness was even stronger in here, he noticed. He held the door back and gestured for Catherine to look.

They carried on up the next staircase, treading on the outer edges of the steps to lessen the sound and came to another landing which looked identical to the first. Salter was about to look into one of the rooms when he stopped.

At the far end of the landing, a flight of metal steps led up to a trapdoor in the ceiling. He looked at Catherine.

"That must be the loft. Let's take a look".

Catherine gripped his arm. "How do we get out of there in a hurry if something goes wrong? Those steps may be the only way in and out. We'd be stuck".

"We've got to see what's up there. Whatever it is, it could tell us what we need to know".

Catherine took hold of his hand, and nodded with a look of resignation.

The metal steps were solid and stable. They steadied themselves with the handrail as they climbed. Halfway up, Salter gestured for them to stop and listen. There was no sound. They continued climbing. At the top of the steps, Salter tested the trapdoor with his finger, then when it didn't move he put his hand against it. It was large and the opening looked wide enough to climb through without much effort. It must be on hinges, he thought. He pushed gently.

Suddenly the trapdoor gave way and opened. He lifted it

slowly until it was vertical, then he grasped the edge with one hand and let it down onto the floor of the loft. He leaned back against the steps and took a deep breath. Catherine reached up and squeezed his hand, smiling reassuringly. He signalled for them to continue.

Just inside the opening, a metal rail was bolted to the floor. Salter took hold of it and pulled himself up. Catherine followed. It was dark.

"Must be a light switch somewhere" whispered Catherine.

"There" said Salter, pointing to the adjacent wall. Catherine reached out and flicked the switch down. What happened took them completely by surprise.

Rows of small angled spotlights mounted on rods hung from the sloping ceiling bathed the whole room in brilliant light. Simultaneously they blinked and rubbed their eyes. Catherine pointed to the trapdoor, indicating for Salter to close it. He followed the instruction. Then they looked around the room, every inch of it illuminated now by the harsh glow of the spotlights.

"Blimey" said Catherine. "Look at this lot".

To their left, one complete wall had been made into a workshop. A wooden bench ran the length of it with a variety of tools scattered untidily over its surface. Extension leads were plugged into sockets and hung down onto the floor, tangled with coils of multi-coloured electrical wire. Adjustable lamps were positioned at points up and down the bench and above it power tools hung on racks.

On the opposite side, laptops and telephones stood on trestle tables. A fax machine stood on a small table by itself. Laminated maps were fixed to the wall and a large pin board was covered in a jumble of A4 sheets. Folding chairs were pushed up against the tables.

But there eyes were drawn to the centre of the room. And their gaze was now fixed on what they saw there.

"My God" said Salter in a hushed whisper.

They walked either side of the three objects that stood in the centre of the room, supported on tubular metal frames. Salter reached his hand out towards the nearest one and ran the tips of his fingers over the light grey paintwork. For a few seconds he just stared, not moving his hand.

"So they're into model aircraft" said Catherine. She looked at him with a puzzled expression.

"These aren't model aircraft". He ran his hand down one of the wings.

"They're UAV's"

"They're what?"

"Unmanned Aerial Vehicles. The Americans have been using them for a few years now. They're still in process of development. I've got a nasty feeling these are a smaller and more advanced version".

Catherine crouched down and looked at the underneath of the one nearest her.

"Yes, I've heard of them, now I think of it. I've never been quite clear about what they do".

"Anything you like. Surveillance maybe. Or they can deliver a payload of bombs. And I'll bet that's what these are for".

He looked around the room, then walked over to the skylights. He looked at each one carefully. Then he turned to Catherine.

"Notice anything funny about the windows?"

She walked across the room and stood beside him.

"Listen". With the knuckles of one hand he tapped on the expanse of wall between two of the skylights. "Sounds hollow, doesn't it?"

Catherine nodded, biting her lower lip.

"What else strikes you?" said Salter.

"Well, they look a bit ... "

"Amateur? Like the whole job was done in a hurry? Like whoever did it didn't care about the finish? Look at the wood around the frames. Rough. Splintered. Not even sanded, let alone painted".

"I see what you mean. It looks sort of like ... "

"It wasn't even meant to last. A temporary job. Now look where I'm pointing". And with his forefinger he pointed to the top edge of each of the three skylights in turn.

"Can you see it?"

"Yes I can. There's a crack in the plaster. It runs right across".

"Exactly. And the same underneath if you look. They're joined together to make one complete section of the wall. Or rather the roof. The whole thing's made to come out in a split second leaving a gaping hole in the roof".

He jerked his thumb back towards the centre of the room.

"And that's where those things go. Straight out of the hole".

Catherine closed her eyes. "Bloody hell!"

"Hampstead's north, right?" said Salter.

"Right".

"Which means we're looking south. Can't you see? They're aimed at Central London! And God only knows what they'll be carrying!"

They stared at each other as the truth of it all sank in.

"But just a minute" said Catherine. "Are you sure these things are big enough for that? You said yourself these are smaller than regular UAV's. I seriously thought they were model aircraft. Those wings can't be more than a couple of metres across. Even if they are more advanced, where do they carry the explosives? I mean, the body must be full of electronic stuff used to guide it. That's probably what that bulge at the front end is. So where do the bombs go? Unless they strap them underneath. And there's a limit to the weight a thing of that size can carry".

Salter looked again at the three objects suspended there, sinister and threatening, their wings swept back like evil birds in flight.

"Who said they carry conventional explosives? Suppose these people have got their hands on something worse. Some kind of tactical nuclear weapon. No-one knows how big those things are. For all we know they could be pocket size. Then these toy airplanes could carry a stack of them".

"This isn't real".

"I'm afraid it is. We could be looking at a nuclear explosion in the middle of London".

They took hold of each other's hands and stood in silence.

"The whole thing would be set off by remote control" said Catherine.

Salter nodded. "With the right sort of equipment, they could be anywhere. Maybe not even in the country. They've probably got explosives up there in the ceiling. The windows would just blow out and those things would be on their way. They'd hit the centre in minutes. Whatever these bastards were planning to do on the Underground, it'd look like a kids' firework party next to this".

"We've got to tell someone. And quick. There's no way of

knowing when it's planned for. It could all go off at any time".

"No argument there".

"God, the police aren't going to believe this".

"In the present climate they probably will".

"So it's back the way we came. We'll have to be careful. We still don't know who's around".

"You're right. Okay, we're out of here" said Salter.

"I don't think so" said the voice of the man who called himself Stefanov Anderek.

Chapter 28

"You're an awkward customer, Father Salter. You disappear just when you're needed most. Then when you're not wanted you turn up out of nowhere".

Anderek, Yanik and a third man had appeared through a door next to one of the trestle tables. Each of them held a gun. Oddly, Salter found himself looking at the door. It had escaped his attention because it blended almost invisibly into the wall, which he now realised was a partition. Anderek walked slowly across the room, his gun pointed at them. He was wearing blue denim jeans and a military-style khaki shirt with patch pockets and epaulettes.

"Who's your friend, by the way? We spotted her when you came into St Pancras".

"My name is Catherine Laurence, if you really need a formal introduction".

Salter heard the contempt in her voice and hoped that Anderek wouldn't react to it.

"You were lucky to find us" said Anderek. "I told Yanik to make sure he wasn't being followed and he messed up. But it doesn't matter now, because your luck has just run out, big time. This house has been our organisation's London base for several months. And it has a very effective and very discreet security system. No-one can just walk in here without the sensors picking them up, however softly they tread. It was amusing watching your progress on the monitor. I bet you never saw the cameras. They are so well hidden".

"The authorities know all about you and your organisation, you know" said Salter.

"Yes I'm sure you've had a nice cosy chat with them" said Anderek in a sneering tone. "We guessed that your arrest was just a performance for our benefit. But we're much too big and too clever to be worried by a bunch of policemen. The small amount of information that these authorities of yours have on our organisation makes no difference to us at all. Wherever we are in the world, we're always one step ahead of them".

"And what about the London Underground? They found out about that".

"That was, as you English would say, a 'red herring'. Oh yes, we would have gone ahead with it. But it was only stage one of the operation. We were quite happy to sacrifice it. The fact that they discovered it has put them off the scent and now we are free to get on with the real business".

Salter felt an almost uncontrollable fear spreading over him. He clenched his hands.

"So what do you plan to do with us?"

"I'm sure you could work that out for yourself, my dear Father. Do you think we'd just let you and your girlfriend walk off now you've seen this place?"

"How do you know we haven't called the police? They could be on their way here right now".

Anderek laughed. It was the laugh Salter remembered from the day he had met him in Hadleigh Bridge.

"You certainly don't give up easily, I'll give you that! The police have nothing on this place, or they would have been here long before now. And somehow I don't think you would have gone sniffing around and putting yourselves in danger if you'd thought the police were just behind you. Even a hero like you wouldn't have risked that. You'd have just let them go in and do the job".

Anderek raised a hand and gestured to the other two. They crossed the room and stood either side of him, still pointing the guns.

"Make one wrong move and your deaths will be even more unpleasant than they would have been otherwise. Now follow me".

Anderek turned and walked back towards the door through which he had come. Yanik and the other man stood back. Salter reached out to take Catherine's hand.

"Keep your hands by your sides where we can see them" said Yanik in a low and menacing voice.

On the other side of the door, they descended a crude staircase made of metal plates and girders bolted together. The room on the floor below had also been partitioned off, so that the staircase was completely concealed. Anderek opened a door in the partition and they followed him through.

They were in one of the small rooms leading off the back staircase. It was full of the emptiness smell. Once again they were stepping on bare floorboards and the floor was strewn with cardboard boxes of different sizes and wooden packing cases. There were no windows and as Anderek flicked a switch on the wall, a single light bulb hanging from the ceiling came on.

"Sit over there" said Anderek indicating folding chairs on the far side of the room.

Catherine stepped in front of Salter and turned her head as if she were about to speak. As she did so, she stumbled against one of the wooden packing cases and fell to the floor with a scream. Then she groaned and rolled on her side.

"Catherine!" said Salter and reached out to her.

"Stay where you are" said the third man and Salter felt the cold metal of a gun barrel against his temple.

"She's hurt, for Christ's sake!"

"I don't give a shit! Stand still or I'll blow your brains out!"

"It's alright Gavin" said Catherine, wincing with pain. "I've just bruised my knee. I think I can get up alright".

"You'd better" said the third man. "Or you won't have any knees".

Salter was straining every muscle in his body with the effort not to move. More than anything else, he wanted some means of killing these three evil creatures. The impulse was strange. He'd never thought that he would want to kill someone.

Catherine got up slowly from the floor, rubbing the palm of her hand over her right knee. With obvious difficulty she walked a few paces, then sat on one of the chairs. Salter pulled a chair up next to her. She smiled at him.

"It's alright. It doesn't really hurt now".

"Get something to tie them up with" said Anderek. Yanik went out of the door to the back staircase and they heard the sound of his feet on the stairs as he went down to the floor below. Anderek and the third man were still pointing their guns.

"So, did you have an interesting talk with the police, Father

Salter?" said Anderek. "I imagine the inside of a police station is not somewhere you are too familiar with".

They had obviously not trailed the van to MI6 headquarters, Salter noted. He felt empowered by this gap in their knowledge. It was like discovering a chink in armour that was otherwise impenetrable.

"Like I said, they'd already found out about the Underground".

"As if it matters now. When we've finished, they'll have more to worry about than how a few commuters get to work. Of course we overheard your conversation upstairs. I think you realise what our little gadgets are designed to do. And well done by the way on the tactical nuclear weapons. That's exactly what we've got. They fit into the body of the aircraft without much trouble and they weigh practically nothing. And of course they are electronically controlled and programmed to go off once the UAV's reach their target. They will strike the City and two further points in the vicinity of Bloomsbury and Hammersmith at roughly the same time late morning, thus leaving a trail of destruction from east to west across London. These nuclear devices are far ahead of their time. Better than anything even the Americans have got. Their capacity is out of all proportion to their size and their capability is ... "

He stopped.

"What the hell is your problem?"

Catherine was sitting with one leg crossed over the other, leaning forward and rocking backwards and forwards in the chair. Her eyes were tightly closed and she seemed to be clutching herself with one hand.

"I wouldn't expect you to understand" she hissed through

gritted teeth. "I'm suffering from a woman's problem". She screwed her eyes up again and drew her breath in sharply.

Salter felt desperation welling up inside him.

"For God's sake, can't you let me do something to help her?"

Anderek lifted the gun and pointed it straight at Salter's face.

"Move one inch off that chair and it'll be the end of your life. I'm not interested in her women's problems. My problem right now is you and I'll solve it this very moment if you don't do as you're fucking well told!" His voice rose to a shrill pitch and the hand holding the gun started to tremble.

"I'm fine" said Catherine, letting her breath out slowly as she spoke. "It's going off now. I'll be alright".

Salter looked at her, trying to say with his eyes everything he wanted to say.

Yanik came back into the room carrying a length of rope. Anderek seemed calmer. He turned his head to look at Yanik.

"What are you? A boy scout? Why didn't you bring some handcuffs?"

"We don't have any" said Yanik in a flat tone.

Anderek shook his head. The hand holding the gun dropped to his side.

"You're a bunch of amateurs. Anyway, it'll have to do. Tie their hands up. But not too tight. We want them to talk".

"Put your hands behind the chair" said Yanik. Salter complied and glanced sideways at Catherine. She still had a pained expression on her face, but she had uncrossed her legs. She did as Yanik said.

"Alright" said Anderek. "Now let's get down to business. You two sit over there. But keep your guns out. We've had trouble with him before and we don't want to take any risks. Not this close to the operation".

He sat down on one of the chairs and stuck his gun into the waistband of his jeans. Then he looked at Salter.

"I want to know exactly and in every detail what you told the police".

"Why should I tell you anything at all?" said Salter.

Anderek looked at the floor. Then he looked up again.

"Quite simply, my dear Father Salter, you should tell me what I want to know in order to make your own death and that of your friend here just a little more bearable. I could dispatch you both very quickly and believe me I'd be doing you a favour. On the other hand, I could subject you to such unbelievable pain and suffering and stretch it out for so long that you would literally be begging me to kill you. Do not for one minute doubt that I can do exactly what I say. I have plenty of experience in this field. In fact I think I am what would be called an expert".

Anderek stared at him and Salter stared back. He must not allow himself to be broken by this, he thought.

"You see, Father Salter, I don't have any of these peculiar hang-ups that you have about the sanctity of human life. And I don't mind inflicting pain to get what I want. In fact I quite enjoy it. It gives me satisfaction. I have no morals or principles or whatever it is you preach about. These things are for the little people. For the weak ones. Those who don't have the strength to take what they want".

He paused again to stare at Salter.

"I'll have no hesitation in making things very unpleasant indeed for you and this bitch of yours. So you had better get on the right side of me. Who knows, I might just show you the very smallest amount of compassion, as I believe you call it".

Salter was still staring back at him, refusing to let him think he was winning. He had often wondered how he would feel if he had to face immanent death. He was surprised at the strength he was finding within himself.

Anderek stood up. He pulled the gun out of the waistband and examined it carefully, turning it over in his hand. He did this with something akin to fascination, as if he were seeing it for the first time. A subtle form of intimidation, thought Salter. Then he replaced the gun and started walking slowly backwards and forwards.

"So let us begin. What did you tell the police?" He spoke without looking at Salter.

"Very little that they didn't already know. I told you they knew about the planned attack on the Underground. They wanted to know why I had agreed to go out to Slovakia. And they wanted to know why I had become suspicious and left Bratislava in such a hurry".

Anderek was still walking backwards and forwards. Salter continued. He was quite certain that Anderek fully intended to kill them both and he was aware that he and Catherine were probably living the last few moments of their life. But strangely something was telling him to play for time.

"I told them about the Institute for Historical and Cultural Research. I also told them that I had visited what appeared to be the Institute's website and that I had exchanged emails with someone claiming to be a member of staff".

"And what specific questions did they ask you about the time you spent in Slovakia?"

Salter waited just a few seconds before answering.

"If what the authorities know makes no difference to you and your organisation, why is it so important for you to know what I told them?"

Anderek stopped where he was and his hand came to rest on the butt of the gun. Then he continued slowly walking.

"You appear to consider inquisitiveness to be some kind of virtue, Father Salter. I can assure you that in your situation it is not. Now I would suggest you answer my question".

Something odd had crept into Anderek's whole bearing and it could be heard in the tone of his voice. At first, Salter couldn't identify what it was. Then he realised. It was patience. Instead of threatening and using physical force, Anderek was trying patiently to get as much information as he could from him. And that meant it was important. How much the authorities knew about his organisation and its workings did matter. It mattered to him and perhaps to those above him. If the Slovakian business had been a botched operation, maybe he was trying hard to salvage something out of it. And maybe he was trying to save his own skin in the process.

In spite of the rope tied around his wrists and the guns trained on him, this was beginning to feel to Salter like a poker game. And it was time for him to play what might just prove to be a very important card.

"Whatever I may have told them, they already know a lot more than you or anyone in your organisation realises".

Anderek's pace seemed to quicken slightly. He had been stepping lightly on the bare floorboards. Now the heels of his shoes were clicking.

"You persist in being evasive. I would advise you to answer the question".

"They certainly told me a few interesting things. For example, they know that your real name is not Anderek. Your name is Jurinko Valach".

Chapter 29

Anderek spun around to face Salter. His whole body was suddenly tense and his fists were clenched. The muscles in his neck were taut, veins stood out on his forehead and his eyes blazed.

"You are playing the wrong game with the wrong person! I have already warned you what your last few minutes on this earth will be like if you do not co-operate!"

Again the voice was shrill. Salter felt intimidated by the display of seething anger. But he also knew he had struck a raw nerve.

"I'm not in the least interested to know what these pathetic bureaucrats have found out about me!"

But he obviously was, thought Salter.

"They can sniff around all they like! They don't know who they are dealing with! We are professionals! Not second-rate civil servants! Our organisation will always have the upper hand over useless pieces of shit like them! And very shortly now, I will be pressing the button that will bring destruction upon their capital city! And there is nothing anyone can do to stop it!"

Anderek pulled the gun out again and for a moment Salter

thought that was it for him and Catherine. But he held it aloft, still staring straight at Salter. And Salter noticed that he seemed to be trying to regain control of himself.

He placed the gun on the seat of the chair. The he started the walking routine again, his thumbs in the pockets of his jeans, his shoulders hunched slightly forwards. Although he seemed calmer, the tension in his body was unmistakeable.

"So, if you reckon they know so much about us, what else did they tell you?"

Back to the poker game, thought Salter. And it struck him that he might have more cards than he had so far realised.

"They know all about the American connection. And they know that Geneva is a front for whatever else the organisation does".

That's it, thought Salter. Nice and vague. It should keep him guessing and wind him up a bit. Nothing to lose anyway.

For a split second Anderek froze. Then he continued walking.

"And what exactly is this American connection?"

Once again Salter waited a moment before answering. He quickly glanced at Catherine out of the corner of his eye. Her head was down, her chin resting on her chest, her eyes closed.

"They didn't tell me much. Why should they? Just that your organisation is owned by some very rich and powerful people in the States. No more than that".

Salter was satisfied with his carefully crafted answer. In a normal situation, he might have been congratulating himself on his skilful use of words. The shadowy American billionaire had become an indeterminate group of people, number unknown. The picture he'd painted was deliberately indistinct. And that would have raised questions in Anderek's mind. What do they know and how much do they know?

Anderek reached into one of the pockets of his shirt and took out a packet of Marlboro and a lighter. Was Salter imagining it or did he fumble as he took the cigarette out of the packet and lit it?

He took a long draw on the cigarette and inhaled the smoke deep into his lungs. Then he turned to face Salter.

"They know nothing, these authorities of yours. At least nothing which would be of any use to them".

Sounds like he's trying to convince himself, thought Salter. "You can't be sure of that" said Salter. The ropes were beginning to cut into his hands, but he steeled himself against the pain, determined not to show it on his face. "They obviously have networks of information stretching from America into Europe".

Anderek's lips twisted into a wry smile.

"Even so, they have nothing they could use against us. We are always ahead of their game".

Time to play another card, Salter decided.

"Do you know what happened to your man in Vienna?"

Anderek was about to take another draw on the cigarette, but his hand stopped in mid-air.

"Someone killed him before he could dispose of you. That was fortunate for you, wasn't it?" Then he lifted his hand to his mouth and drew heavily on the cigarette.

"He was shot by a British agent who'd been tailing him. And the Austrian police will by now have examined whatever he had on him, including the Russian sniper's rifle he was carrying in his shoulder bag. They will have his finger prints and no doubt other pieces of useful information. All of which will have added to the knowledge they have".

Of course it was all bluff. There was no guarantee that a dead assassin's finger prints would have told the authorities anything at all. And he may have been carrying nothing of any interest or value to the Austrian police. But it was meant to give the overall impression that someone out there knew a lot about Anderek's organisation. That they'd been piecing it together slowly, bit by bit, over a period of time. And it was meant to chip away at his sense of security. If he was being held to account for the failure of the operation in its early stages, it would increase the anxiety he was feeling. And Anderek's reaction told Salter that it had succeeded in doing just that.

The fingers of the hand that held the cigarette tightened until the cigarette was crushed. For a second, he thought Anderek hadn't noticed he'd done it. Then he flung the cigarette to the floor. It rolled across the bare boards and lodged in a crack, its embers still smoking.

"Don't make it hard on yourself!"

The words were forced out from between tightened lips.

"If you think you can do yourself any good by being clever with me, then you are sadly mistaken".

Anderek took a deep breath. Then reaching into his shirt pocket, he took out another cigarette and lit it.

He's wondering what to say next, thought Salter. And he deliberately kept his gaze steady, looking Anderek straight in the eye.

"You asked me what I know and I'm telling you".

There's the ball, back in your court, he thought.

"Very well" said Anderek, and taking another lungful of

smoke he started walking again.

"I'm glad to see you're complying with instructions. Continue to give me the information I require".

Now he's trying to make out he's in charge, thought Salter. In fact he's losing control and he knows it.

His mind went quickly but carefully over the session with Benjamin James, looking for any detail he could use that would strike a chord.

"They know of course about the drug trafficking and the arms shipments".

"So what? The international drugs trade's too big for any country's authorities to do anything about. And as for the arms shipments, we often deal with governments. If anyone tried to interfere they'd get their fingers badly burnt".

Salter paused for effect. Just like he did in a sermon, he couldn't help thinking.

"And what about the man at the Gare du Nord? The one with the poison needle. You know they'll be questioning him at this very moment".

Anderek drew on the cigarette, clearly weighing up what he'd just heard.

"They'll get nothing from him. He knows only too well what would happen to him if he gave anything away about us".

"And what if they offered him a new identity and a new life somewhere else in the world in exchange for all the information he had and everything he knew. They could arrange that very easily and very quickly. Your organisation would be badly damaged and there would be nothing they could do about it".

Anderek stopped and turned to face him. For a moment Salter thought he was going to do the cigarette-crushing routine again, but he seemed to be more in control of himself this time.

"He wouldn't even get out of the country. And even if he did, we would be after him wherever he went".

"Can you be so sure? The authorities use that strategy all the time. How would you find out where they'd sent him? Law enforcement has international networks. International crime is haphazard. You would have lost your man completely and I think he knows that. It's certainly what the French police will be telling him. I'll bet he's singing like a lark".

The muscles in Anderek's face were tightening. His eyes were blazing. Now he's worried, thought Salter as he carried on.

"And how much can you really trust these people who work for you? If the poison-needle guy knows about this London base of yours because he's heard about it on the grapevine, he could have already told the French about it". Another bluff, thought Salter. He hoped it would hold. "Which of course means the French will have been in contact with London. It may only be a matter of time".

There was a move to Salter's left. It was the third man. He had taken a pace forward.

"What's he saying?"

He sounded agitated and for the first time, Salter looked at him closely. He was young, early twenties at the most. The voice was slightly high-pitched and the accent was standard South London. He was thin with dark eyes and pointed features and his greasy, unkempt hair was cut short. He was dressed in close-fitting black trousers and a black jacket, and the grubby white shirt was open at the neck. He seemed not to have the same confident bearing the other two had and he fingered the gun as if he were nervous of it. Salter guessed he was a new recruit to this business. The apprentice thug. The learner. The one who'd get ordered around and given the menial jobs.

"You said this'd be alright! You said we'd be out of here and on a plane when the job was done! If the police know about this place, we're fucked! We'll all be dead!"

Even from where he was, Salter could see the beads of sweat on the man's forehead.

"Shut up Connor!" said Yanik. It was the first time his name had been used, Salter noted.

"Pull yourself together!" said Anderek, almost screaming. "He's talking that shit to wind us up! Can't you see that? The police know nothing! In a few minutes these two will be dead! We will complete this task as we have been ordered to do!"

"How do you know the police don't know anything? If the guy in Paris knew about the London base, the police could've got it out of him! Just like this geezer says! How do you know they haven't? They could be on their way here now! They could even be surrounding the place! We gotta get out!"

"We stay and we finish the job" said Anderek. Salter noticed he was using the same measured enunciation and slow menacing tone he had used when speaking to them.

"Yeah? Who says?" Connor was holding his gun in both hands now. He had begun visibly to tremble. "For all you know we could 'ave minutes! Then we could be shooting it out with armed coppers! And they'll have serious hardware! Not just these bloody peashooters! You must be fuckin' mental! This whole thing's crazy anyway! We can't pull this off! Nobody could! You lot can get splattered up the walls if you like! I wanna life and I'm out of it!" He was breathing fast now. Almost hyperventilating, Salter noticed. And his speech was becoming more and more animated.

He raised the gun, still holding it with both hands, and pointed it directly at Anderek.

"Tell him to drop his gun! And don't even think of touchin' yours!"

Anderek gave one nod of his head in Yanik's direction and Yanik's gun fell to the floor.

"Kick it over 'ere!" said Connor. Yanik obeyed and Connor went down slowly onto one knee, keeping his own gun trained on Anderek, and picked Yanik's gun up, slipping it into his left jacket pocket.

"Now back off!" Anderek took three paces backwards and Connor stepped forward and took the gun from the seat of the chair, putting it into the same pocket.

"Raise y' hands slowly and put them behind y' head". Anderek and Yanik complied, slowly and mechanically, in unison. The cigarette fell from Anderek's fingers onto the floor.

"Now what you do with these two is y'own business. But don't try and follow me. I got the guns and I'll use 'em".

Salter felt the tension in the room creeping into his body as he watched the strange scene being played out in front of him. Some kind of possibility was emerging. Just the slimmest chance. If they tried to jump Connor before he got out, he might just kill one of them. Maybe both. Even if one of them was dead or injured, he and Catherine might somehow overcome the other one. His hands were tied but they weren't tied to the chair. He could get free of it. Then at least he could use his legs. Wait now. Just wait. Try to be calm.

Connor was walking backwards in the direction of the door to the metal staircase. He was moving slowly on the balls of his feet, the gun still pointing straight at Anderek. As he came level with Yanik, he stopped.

"Back off and get over there!" As he spoke, he inclined his head towards the far corner of the room.

Yanik was motionless.

"I said back off and get over there!" He raised his voice and the words were strained as the muscles in his throat tightened.

Yanik stayed perfectly still.

"Fuckin' do it or he gets it and so do you!" Connor's whole body was now shaking and the sweat from his forehead began to run down the side of his face.

Salter almost missed the next thing that happened. It was done in a split second. Yanik's left hand was suddenly holding a knife. The gleaming blade, at least six inches long, flashed a reflection of the light from the single electric bulb. Then his hand was behind Connor's back.

The gun slipped from Connor's fingers and clattered on the wooden floorboards at his feet. His mouth fell open and his wide eyes stared blankly.

Almost as quickly, Yanik pulled the blade out of Connor's back and switched the blood-soaked knife to his right hand. Then with a single thrust he buried the blade in Connor's stomach. Connor's eyes glazed over and he crumpled to the floor.

Yanik knelt down beside Connor's body and unbuttoned the jacket. Then he wiped the knife on Connor's white shirt, carefully removing all traces of the blood and examining the blade when he had finished. With his cold disinterest and fixed expression, he might have been washing up after preparing a meal. He replaced the knife in the sheath concealed in the right sleeve of his jacket from which it had come and retrieved the guns from Connor's pocket. Walking over to the chair, he placed Anderek's gun where it had been. Then he walked back across the room and resumed his standing position, the gun in his right hand, as if nothing had happened.

"You must think you are very clever, Father Salter. If you were destined to live a long life you could tell your grandchildren how skilfully you bluffed your way out of certain death. However, as we both know, your life is going to be very short indeed and your undoubted powers of persuasion will die with you".

Salter had never been in any doubt that he was confronted by ruthless and cold-blooded killers who were unquestioningly following orders, who would stop at nothing and whose immediate intention was to end his life and Catherine's. But for the briefest moment there had been a ray of hope that the situation might somehow change to their advantage. That had now gone. It had disappeared as quickly as it had appeared. And the only question now, it seemed, was how to die.

He glanced at Catherine. She was still sitting perfectly still, her eyes closed and her head forward. She looked oddly relaxed. As he thought about everything that had passed between them in the last few days, he wanted to thank her. And then he wanted to apologise to her for being the cause of what would now be a useless and tragic death for them both.

Anderek took the cigarettes out of his shirt pocket again and lit one. He inhaled the smoke luxuriously, then exhaled it from his nostrils.

"So let's continue where we left off, shall we? What are you going to say to make me spare you unnecessary suffering? What could you tell me that would make me a little more kindly disposed towards you?"

So he was still fishing to see if he could find out more, thought Salter. He must really feel under pressure from somewhere to patch things up. Or maybe it was an ego thing. He'd really flipped when he found out the authorities knew his real name. Maybe he needed to see himself as this mysterious figure, cloaked in secrecy, untouchable, beyond the reach of justice. And maybe he panicked if anything threatened to dent that image.

"Why should I have anything else to tell you?"

A slightly puzzled look crossed Anderek's face. He stared hard at Salter, then drew on the cigarette again.

"So, are you not going to ask for mercy, so that you can at least die with dignity?"

"And what would someone like you know about mercy?"

Anderek laughed. "Well you are certainly putting on a brave face. One must admire you for that".

He dropped the cigarette onto the floor and extinguished it with the heel of one shoe. Then he picked up the gun.

"There was a time when those skilled in the art of torture were venerated. Emperors and generals would seek them out and pay them well for their services. Now the world is run by people like you with your bourgeois morality and your social consciences. And you cannot even begin to appreciate the genius of someone like myself".

Not just evil. Mad as well, thought Salter.

"I know more about the workings of the human body than any doctor. All your stupid medics can do is give the dregs of the human race a bit more life and keep them going for a bit longer, when most of them would be better off dead anyway. But what I can do is to inflict such excruciating pain that my victims lose the very will to stay alive. I can deprive them of everything except an all-pervading longing for death. Whatever delusions they may once have had about the meaning of life, life will no longer have any meaning for them at all because their life will have been reduced to unbearable agony. The only thing that will have any meaning will be death. Because only death can put an end to what they are suffering".

"And what if you fail to do all that?"

"I do not fail".

"But how would you know that you had succeeded?"

"You talk nonsense".

"No, it isn't nonsense. It's clearly something you've never thought about. You are assuming that when you kill me, you'll have taken away from me any hope I might have had or any sense of the meaning of life. But how will you know if you have succeeded in doing that? How will you know what is going on in my mind in the last few minutes of my life? Are you expecting me to tell you?"

Anderek's hand tightened around the gun.

"Do you think I have the patience to listen to this stupidity? I could kill you now without a second's hesitation!"

"You could. But then that would be doing the very opposite of what you said you intended to do".

Anderek slowly lowered the gun until his arm hung at his side.

"So you regard what I have said as nothing more than an empty threat. And you doubt that I would carry it out". The words were full of menace.

"No, I don't doubt in the least that a psychopath like you would do exactly as you have said to one of your victims. I am only asking you how you'd know whether you'd achieved your aim. Because unless you knew for certain that you'd succeeded in doing what you'd set out to do, there would for ever be the possibility that you'd failed".

Once again, Anderek's face was taut and veins appeared on his forehead.

"I do not fail".

"But how can you be sure of that?"

"You will realise that I do not fail".

"Now you're making assumptions again. You're assuming that whatever you inflict on me will overcome my resistance".

"You have no resistance that is strong enough to withstand what I will do to you".

"But you don't know that. And once I have died, it will be impossible for you ever to find out whether you were right or not. And that means there will always be the possibility that you had failed".

"So you think you are stronger than I am!" The tension building up within him was raising the pitch of his voice and his face was turning red.

"I may be and I may not be. But how will you ever know once I'm dead? And if it turns out that I am stronger than you are, then you've failed".

Anderek turned and walked two paces. Then with a violent swing of his right leg he kicked one of the folding chairs. It skidded across the boards and tipped onto its side, coming to rest a few feet away.

He spun around to face Salter, raising the gun. But instead

of aiming it he seemed to be brandishing it like a blunt instrument. It was close to being a gesture of exasperation.

"Who exactly do you think you are? And what makes you think you can get the better of me? You are nothing but a self-appointed peddler of virtue! You don't have the courage to look at yourself and see that your life and everything in it is worthless! All you can do is console yourself with a load of stupid fairy tales! You are nothing more than an insect that is destined to be stamped on and destroyed! The world belongs to those of us who have the power to get what we want! And when insects like you get in our way, we will trample on them until none of them is left! Then maybe the world will begin to learn what true greatness is!"

Salter had begun to wonder where this was leading. Anderek was ranting like some deranged dictator who had just pulled off a military coup. But it was also as if he was engaging him in a kind of debate. And Salter realised that Anderek needed him to give in and admit defeat. As if his evil and twisted self-esteem depended on it. Was it possible that Salter had managed to gain the upper hand? And if so, for how long?

From somewhere in the distance came the droning of an engine.

Yanik had been standing motionless like a dummy in a shop window. Now he threw himself across the room in the direction of the window like a runner off the starting blocks. He took hold of one of the net curtains delicately between his forefinger and thumb and drew it back by a few centimetres.

"Helicopter" he said in the flat tone.

"So what the hell is it and what's it doing? The others will be on their way here soon. If that's the police snooping we need to warn them". Anderek put the gun into the waistband of his jeans and walked across the room to join Yanik at the window. The droning was louder now. The helicopter was getting closer.

"Do we call them?" said Yanik.

"Wait" said Anderek. "It may be nothing. Watch it and see what it does".

Salter strained his neck to look at the window but it was impossible to see anything through the thick fabric of the net. Then he turned to look at Catherine and she looked back at him. She mouthed something. He didn't understand what she was saying and he peered at her, his brow creased. She mouthed the words again and he realised she had said 'Just keep calm'.

"It's overhead, I can see it" said Yanik.

"It's moving away" said Anderek. "It looks like it's doing traffic observation or something like that. Nothing to worry us".

The two of them stood at the window looking through the gap in the net curtain. The sound of the helicopter seemed to be further away. Then for a few seconds it was closer. Finally it receded into the distance. Then the sound was gone.

Anderek walked back across the room and resumed his position. He looked more relaxed and his face was its normal colour. He seemed to have regained control.

"We must not waste any more time". He gestured to Yanik. "Get some more rope and tie them securely to the chairs so they cannot move. I want to get this over with quickly now".

Yanik left the room and returned with a further length of rope. Producing what looked like a wooden-handled pruning knife from his jacket pocket, he proceeded to cut the rope into a number of pieces. Then he tied Salter's legs and arms to the chair. This time, Salter noticed, he spared him no pain or discomfort but pulled the rope tight. The time for talking was obviously over. He did the same to Catherine.

Salter looked at her and she smiled back at him. It was the smile he'd seen so often in the last few days. A smile that made him feel warm and comforted and secure. A smile that made him love her. He desperately wanted to say something but found he couldn't speak. And then he remembered the many occasions on which he'd taught people that silence could be worth more than a thousand words. Maybe this was what he had always meant, whether he realised it or not.

Yanik had finished his sadistic task and walked back across the room and once again took up his statue-like posture. Anderek took out the gun and checked the magazine.

"Why not try praying to your God, Father Salter. Perhaps he will make your death more bearable. I certainly have no intention of doing so. You have seen fit to doubt what I am capable of doing to you and your woman. Well you are about to find out. As they say, there is no substitute for experience. It only remains for me to decide which one of you to deal with first. Perhaps the choice should be yours. Which of you would like to watch the horrific death of the other?" And he laughed in a sneering tone.

"Curse you, you evil bastard!" Salter hissed the words between his teeth. "You'll pay for this somehow! Don't ever doubt that!"

"More of your childish fables? I don't think they'll give you much comfort now. It is simply for me to ... "

A crashing noise of splintering wood filled the air as the two doors of the room flew open. Two figures dressed from head to foot in black, their faces partially covered by balaclavas, appeared in the doorways. Yanik turned and raised his gun. A single shot rang out and he spun around clutching his shoulder and dropping the gun.

Anderek aimed in the direction from which the shot had come. But he never pulled the trigger. Instead, his whole body suddenly convulsed in a macabre dance as a hail of machine gun bullets hit him.

Then Jurinko Valach, who had called himself Stefanov Anderek, folded slowly to the floor and rolled over. Crimson patches began to flower on his khaki shirt. His eyes stared blankly into infinity.

"I thought I said I didn't want to see you two again" said Benjamin James.

Chapter 30

Five men in black were now in the room. They had all removed their balaclavas. One of them was applying a makeshift bandage to Yanik's shoulder, while another radioed for medical help. Another examined the two bodies and confirmed they were both dead.

Meanwhile two of them had cut the ropes. Salter stood up, unsteadily at first, rubbing the welts that had appeared on his wrists and stretching his legs. He turned to Catherine and put his arms around her. She rested her head on his shoulder.

"Are you alright?"

"Yes I'm fine". She looked at him and grinned broadly. He was surprised by the unexpected brightness of her expression.

"All clear upstairs then?" said James.

"Yes sir. There's no-one else around" replied one of the men. "But you might like to take a look at what's up there".

"I can't wait". James raised his eyebrows quizzically.

"I suppose you were in the helicopter" said Salter.

James nodded.

"Our pilot flew around a couple of times just to confuse them. She's pretty experienced at doing that. Then we did a lightning drop in someone's garden a few doors up. The poor folk must still be recovering from the shock".

"So how did you know we'd be here? I guess you must have been following us".

"No, we had no idea where you'd gone after you left MI6. I figured it was none of our business. In any case, I was thinking you'd chill out for a day or two then go quietly home. I didn't reckon on you getting tied up with this lot again. But it wasn't too hard to pinpoint you once the direction finder got to work. We've got the very latest hardware, as you might expect. But that's a state secret, of course".

Salter looked at him. "But I don't understand. You say, direction finder. Surely you had to have something to home in on, otherwise we could have been anywhere".

"That's right. We homed in on the signal from your mobile once you made the call. How did you manage to do that, by the way? That must have been bloody difficult with those characters watching you all the time".

"But I didn't make a phone call! How could I possibly have done?"

"I did" said Catherine.

Salter looked at her.

"What are you talking about? When did you make a phone call?"

Catherine smiled. She lifted the hem of her skirt up to her waist and thrust her hand between her legs. Her hand reappeared holding her mobile.

Salter shook his head. "But I still don't understand! What the hell did you do?"

"Do you remember when we came in here from the room upstairs and I fell over the packing case?"

"I certainly do!" said Salter. "I was really worried you'd hurt yourself!"

"That's what I wanted them to think. When I appeared to be writhing around in agony, I was actually taking the mobile out of my skirt pocket and shoving it down the front of my underwear. I had to make it secure before I got up again in case it fell out. These lacy things aren't really made for holding a mobile. So I spun the whole thing out for a while to give myself time".

Salter was standing open-mouthed.

"But how on earth did you manage to use it?"

"Well, when I was pretending to have what I called women's problems, I was dialling the number on the card Benjamin had given us. I put the number in my contacts folder at the hotel last night. I thought it was best in case we ever needed it. I'm hopeless with bits of card. I always lose them. Anyway, I'm pretty familiar with the buttons on my mobile. I've had it a while now. So I had no problem finding the contacts by touch. The phone was switched on because I keep it on all the time. And once the folder was open, I just scrolled down to BJ for Benjamin James. It had to be the third one down, because I've only got two A's in it and he's the only B. After that, it was press green for go. I thought if I could at least get through to someone we'd have more of a chance. Maybe give a clue of some kind as to where we were. And I was hoping the call could be traced with all this technology stuff they have these days. Then I just kept very still so they wouldn't take any notice of me".

Benjamin James was shaking his head and laughing.

"I don't believe this, Miss Laurence. That was nothing but sheer brilliance on your part. I think you should come and work for us".

"So what did you guys hear on the other end when you answered?" said Salter.

"Well it wasn't quite like that". James had removed the gold-rimmed glasses and was polishing the lenses with a silk handkerchief. "The number you were given wasn't just any old phone number. It was one of those we ask our agents to use if we are likely to want to track them and they have no other means of contacting us in an emergency. It went in the first place to the tracking room in our communications centre and alerted the boffins there. Our equipment was able to pick up what was going on around you and amplify it. In fact I had it playing through my earphones on the flight here. And your friend Valach was very obliging when he ranted on at such great length and in such a loud voice. That was how we knew you were in trouble of some kind".

Salter turned to Catherine and hugged her again. "You saved our lives".

"So did you" said Catherine. "You kept him going on his ego-trip and it bought us time".

"So what brought you to this place?" said James.

"Him". Salter pointed to Yanik. "He was one of those I met in Slovakia. I saw him on the tube at Knightsbridge and we followed him".

"You've done us a big favour, that's for sure. We didn't know anything about this place. It must be their London base. And I'll bet it's full of useful information".

"How do you reckon they managed to keep it a secret?"

James shrugged. "It's not too hard in a neighbourhood like this one. People round here tend to be taken up with their own affairs or they're away a lot of the time. All they needed to do was have someone walk in and out occasionally and switch a few lights on. The word would soon go round there was some rich recluse living here, or a wealthy foreigner who spent most of the year abroad. Not a problem really".

"It just looked like an empty house to us" said Salter. "That is until we took a look in the loft".

"Yes, my colleague here said something about that, didn't he? I couldn't help wondering what he meant. Tell me it's not what I think it is".

"Worse, probably. In your line of business you'd know more about it than I do. But they've got three UAV's up there and they look pretty well ready to go. And according to what Anderek said, they're carrying battlefield nuclear weapons. A whole section of the roof comes out and they head for three targets across London. The rest you can imagine".

James pursed his lips and whistled softly.

"I'll get someone here right away to disarm them".

"You've got some time but not much" said Salter. "Anderek talked about the others being on their way here. It could be that final preparations are scheduled to take place quite soon. Although obviously their on-site team's in a bad way now".

James grinned broadly.

"You're really picking this up, Father Salter. How are you ever going to go back to your quiet life?"

Catherine giggled. And Salter felt himself being drawn out of the nightmare he had been in and back to the world he and Catherine had begun to make for themselves.

"Alright" said James in a commanding tone of voice. "We'll clear up the mess here and then I'm afraid you'll be taken back to MI6 again. I want a doctor to take a look at you both and there'll be another debriefing. I know it's a drag after what you've just been through, but you'll appreciate you've got some very interesting things to tell us. And it might mean we hit this evil outfit really hard. Much harder than we've hit them so far. After that we'll take you back to wherever you're staying at the moment".

He paused.

"And this time I really don't want to see you again".

Chapter 31

The side street was quiet, except for a few cars trying to escape the traffic on Kensington High Street and there was a slight chill in the air as September began to edge towards Autumn. They sat in the window of the café round the corner from their hotel. Catherine stirred her hot chocolate, then licked the spoon.

The anonymous-looking car had dropped them off early evening. Once in their room, they had fallen into bed and stayed there for an hour or so, feeling the tension lifting from them like a heavy burden. Then they had showered together and found a small restaurant for dinner. They had slept soundly through the night and woken up in each other's arms.

"Do you think we'll ever hear any more of that affair?"

"I sincerely hope not!" said Salter.

"No, I wasn't thinking they might come after us again. I don't think I'd be too keen on that either. What I meant was, I wonder if there'll be any echoes of it all on the news or in the press".

"I'd certainly like to know a bit more about that wealthy nutter in Texas. I'm really dying to know what his name is and what kind of stuff he's into. And what that crazy church outfit he runs is like. We'll just have to keep our eye on the Sunday papers".

Catherine stirred the hot chocolate again.

"Do you think they really understood what they were doing? I mean, I know they were going to nuke London and they must have known what that would do. But if this American guy really wanted to bring on the end of the world, do you think he told Anderek and his thugs about it? Were they going along with his loony ideas? And if they weren't, then what did they think it was all about?"

"Hard to say now. My guess is they were just following orders because that's what they were programmed to do. Anderek was basically a mercenary and they're paid to do the job, not ask questions. And if the Texan's as rich as James says he is, he probably pays his troops well. For all we know they could have retired on the payoff from that job".

Catherine nodded and sipped the hot chocolate.

"I thought James was a bit restrained when we told him about those planes and the bombs? I mean, if it'd happened the way they'd planned it … . But he was really cool about it. Just took it in his stride".

"I thought so too" said Salter. "I reckon he was quietly kicking himself for not knowing they had a London base. He must have felt bad about it. Probably thought he should have been the one to find out, rather than having us stumble on it by chance. It shows you what slick operators these bastards are. Getting their hands on expensive property in London and setting up camp there without anyone knowing what was going on".

He took a mouthful of his coffee.

"And they came very close to fooling me. Too close, in fact. If only I hadn't fallen for that line Anderek was spinning me".

"But they didn't pull it off, did they?" Catherine ran the tip of her forefinger along the back of his hand. "It was you that sussed them out. You know it was. You blew the whole thing completely open".

"Yeah, I guess. They were outside their field. It only took a small technical detail and one person who hadn't done his homework to screw everything up. But apart from that, it was a pretty impressive scam. And I was all set to go for it".

"So you still blame yourself".

Salter leaned back in his chair. "I suppose I do, in a way".

Catherine took hold of his hand and they sat in silence for a moment.

"Right" said Catherine. "Try this for size. Forget about it being a scam. What were you hoping to get out of it?"

"A different sort of life, whatever that might have been. It looked like the sort of opportunity that doesn't come around too often. And I figured if I didn't take it, I'd spend the rest of my days regretting it".

"Exactly. So you can't really blame yourself for going after it, can you?"

"No, I suppose not".

"So no more feeling bad. Alright?"

"Alright". And they sat in silence again.

Catherine spoke.

"So do you want to make any plans before we go back?"

"What sort of plans?"

"About how we're going to handle things. Us being together, I mean".

"No, I don't think so. I'd rather wait till we get there and just see how things go".

Catherine chewed the end of her thumb.

"Do you still want a different sort of life?"

"It *will* be a different sort of life. Because from now on it won't be just me. It'll be us".

"I just hope I can make it exciting enough for you".

Salter looked deep into her eyes.

"You haven't done a bad job so far".

They paid for their drinks and left, walking slowly in the direction of the hotel.

"What's the time?" said Catherine. "I didn't put my watch on".

"It's just after eleven. If we get packed now and catch a cab to Waterloo we'll be in Hadleigh Bridge by mid-afternoon. Time to do a quick bit of shopping, then we can get dinner at my place. And afterwards we can go somewhere and watch the sunset".

"Or we could ride off into it". She looked at him and grinned.

"Just shut up".

He slipped his hand into hers and their fingers intertwined.